ARCHER THORN

THE BLACK CAPE SAGA
BOOK ONE

First edition 2024

Published by Everwatch Books

Book Cover Design and Interior Formatting by 100Covers.

ISBN 979-8-9899620-1-3

For every human on Earth.
Except Amanda.
YOU KNOW WHY, AMANDA.

ONE

SKYPUNCHER saved the world again.

What a jackass.

James Riven flicked a stale piece of popcorn at the TV. The kernel bounced off the hero's perfectly sculpted chin.

"Oops. No snacks for you, Skypuncher," Jim muttered. "That's too bad."

The stupid hero kept jabbering into a dozen microphones, unaware of how deeply and awesomely he'd just been burned.

Jim turned back to his bar and resumed polishing. The long stretch of oak was old and needed lots of TLC. It had character, though, if character meant *should have been replaced a decade ago*.

"It was a challenge at the end, I'll be honest," Skypuncher said. "But I speak for the Spectrum when I tell you proudly that the citizens of the world are safe once again."

Jim couldn't help glancing over his shoulder at the screen. The camera had pulled back, showing off the white costume stretched over Skypuncher's tall, muscular frame. His dark hair had a streak of gray, and it swept back in a way that somehow looked effortless and epic all at once. His yellow cape rippled dramatically despite the total lack of wind. It always did that, sitting or billowing perfectly in every situation.

Big deal. Jim could look like a hero, too, if he wanted. He just . . . uh . . . had to replace his average height and build with a different height and build. And replace his average brown hair with different hair. And be willing to wear a costume. And . . . you know what, looking like a hero is stupid.

Skypuncher was still talking, and the crowd worshipped him. It was plastered all over their faces. Everyone called him the world's truest hero, and he certainly did look the part. But when Jim looked at him, he saw something very different. Something the general masses would never know.

He flicked his finger and the TV switched to a Velocity game. The North American League playoffs had begun, and tonight the Portland Shockwaves were playing the Kansas City Scimitars. Everyone said it should be a great game.

"Aw, Jim, can't you turn that back?" Marissa, a regular, said from her barstool. "I wanna hear how they beat the bad guy. What was his moniker? Sinewave, I think."

Jim gave his best apologetic grin. "Sorry, you know we have a strict No Smarmy Douches rule."

"Come on, he's the best," Marissa said. "Plus, I hear it's more than a victory speech. They're announcing something big."

Jim feigned excitement. "A new flavor of Skypuncher pudding pops?"

"Bigger," she laughed. "It's only a rumor, though. No one really knows."

"Too bad. Personally, I was hoping for bubble gum flavor." Jim gave a theatrical sigh. "Well, never let it be said that I'm not a kind and merciful barman."

He flicked his finger again, a tiny gesture more for himself than any onlookers. A faint zing-spark sensation traveled down his arm, and for an instant there was a connection between himself and the TV. The channel switched back.

"You're the best, Jim," Marissa said. "Another round?"

"You got it."

Ice. Vodka. Juice. Shaker. Glass. One Bay Breeze later, Jim set Marissa's cocktail on the bar as a new customer arrived. Sort of new, anyway.

Stocky, middle-aged black man with a close-cropped beard, wearing a janitor-type jumpsuit. This was his fourth visit in as many weeks, and each time he'd ventured a few tables closer to the bar. Now he stepped right up and slid onto a barstool. Though he still chose a spot with a view of the entire bar, the dining area, the arena, and the exits.

Which reminded Jim, tonight's match needed to start soon. He glanced toward the circular, half-dilapidated arena where his "contenders" were suiting up. That's contenders with air quotes. Sure, they were twice as old as this ancient bar and they mixed fiber pills with their cocktails, but hey, these days, this was their only time to shine.

They didn't need his attention yet, so Jim approached the (hopefully) new regular, careful to look welcoming but not eager. Some customers spooked easily at first.

"Hey there, welcome to Versus. I'm Jim. What can I get you?"

"Eli," the man said in a low, gravelly voice. "Scotch, please. Whatever's cheap."

"You got it."

With practiced ease, Jim chipped a sliver of purified ice from a block and swirled it around the inside of a tumbler. Then he tossed the ice and grabbed a bottle of eighteen-year-old single malt.

"Don't worry, I'll charge you for the bottom shelf stuff," he said as he poured. "But life's too short to drink cheap scotch, and this stuff is smoky enough to change your life." He slid the glass over. "Consider it a nice-to-meet-you."

"Much obliged." Eli tipped the glass in his direction before taking a sip. His eyebrows raised slightly. "Nice."

"Right? I never lie about scotch. Only about tequila, and it knows what it did."

A glance at the arena told Jim it was time to get this started before his fighters crumbled to dust all on their own. Sauntering over to the PA, he palmed the mouthpiece and pressed the button on the side.

"Ladies and gentlemen, it's main event time! Who's excited for a match between two absolute titans?"

A wan, half-hearted cheer went up from the sparse crowd.

Yeah, that seems about right, Jim thought.

He went on to announce the contenders, both semi-well-known locals from long long long loooooooooooooooooong ago. One had been a minor hero, the other a minor villain. They carried a long-standing grudge about some pawn shop heist forty years ago, and insisted on coming back here every few months to settle the score once and for all. Each time, they wore the same threadbare costumes, and tonight was no different.

"And . . . VERSUS!" Jim shouted.

The two has-beens circled each other, throwing wet-noodle punches, looking for openings. There were so many, Jim could have driven a truck through them. Was it possible that they were even slower this time? Shaking his head, he turned his attention back to the bar.

"No referee?" Eli asked.

Jim chuckled. "Not for these guys. It'll be a glorified slap fight until one of them gets a split lip. Then they'll spend the rest of the night drinking together and arguing over who dated Eartha Kitt first. Besides, this bar is a Warded Zone. No one gets really hurt."

He gestured over his shoulder at the small copper shield mounted to the wall, which marked the establishment as a safe area. Fights would only happen by mutual agreement, and no one would fight to kill, or even seriously injure, while in its presence. Any parahuman crossing into the shield's radius would receive a small psionic burst, alerting them telepathically that it was time to behave, and even the worst of them abided by it. For decades, this agreement had been honored by all parahumans, hero and villain alike. Some codes you just don't break.

Eli eyed the shield, then the fighters in the arena. "Time does interesting things to people. To old rivalries."

"Now, that is far too deep and insightful for this bar, sir," Jim said. "I insist you stop making sense and drink more of my scotch instead."

The corner of Eli's mouth quirked up, a hint of a smile. He lifted the glass and sipped.

"What do you do at Atherton?" Jim asked. Eli gave him a questioning glance, so he gestured at the patch on his jumpsuit. "Corporate logo. I see it on the skyscraper when I walk home."

For a moment, Eli seemed to study him. Then he looked away and took another sip. "I work at lots of places. I'm the custodian."

"For a place like that, must be a big job."

Eli didn't respond to the implied question. Instead, he glanced around the bar as if weighing and measuring what he saw. "I dropped in here once, must have been twenty years ago. Back then, it was . . ."

"A lot shinier? Packed to the walls with heroes and villains? Not smelling like dust and regret?" Jim gave a careless shrug. "Yeah, we're the underdog now, I guess. That's our town, classic Highreach. Glamour is more Cloudreach's department, and really, who wants to drink in a city that smells that good?"

Eli wasn't the first to observe the change to the bar. Jim had owned Versus for seven years, but the decline had begun a decade before he'd come around. Long ago, though, this place had been a Highreach institution. The unofficially official bar where heroes and villains of any level would come have a drink, trade some punches, and work out grievances that couldn't be worked out on the streets or in the skies.

Then came a new owner, who saw this place as more of a convenient way to launder money than a cultural cornerstone. Then came the inevitable decline, and the even more inevitable criminal indictment of the owner. Then came Jim, who looked at what Versus had become and saw, not a landmark begging to be revitalized, but a perfect place to do exactly what he wanted–settle into a dark corner of the city and be forgotten.

"Oh, hey, Jim!" Marissa called, waving him over as she gathered her things to leave. When he approached, she leaned across the bar and gave his hand a squeeze. "Thanks for that playlist, by the way. Your remix totally set the mood."

"Oh yeah, that date was coming up, right? With the . . . stock broker?"

"Corporate accountant."

"Scary numbers man, got it. Glad I could help. Let me know if he misbehaves, and I'll give you a terrible track that'll stick in his head until he goes crazy."

Marissa laughed. "Sounds like there's a story behind that one."

"It employs a specific series of notes, and the story of how I found it is, um . . . well, let's just say I shot myself with my own gun. But that stays between friends, right?"

Marissa mimed locking her lips closed and throwing away the key. "Guess the Spectrum isn't announcing anything after all, so I'd better get home. See you next week?"

"I'll be the guy behind the bar." Jim waved as Marissa headed for the exit, then stepped over to check on Eli. "Anything to eat? How about some lukewarm fries covered in cheese of dubious origin?"

"No, thanks. You have some sort of musical power?"

"Nah. I'm just good with stuff that runs on electricity, so I mess around with a synthesizer. Some days get more interesting than others. That particular day, I was . . ."

He trailed off, feeling as if something was wrong but unsure why. Something about the rhythm of this place had changed. He swept his eyes across the space, taking in the details he'd seen ten thousand times before, looking for . . . there it was. A burly man with bushy salt-and-pepper hair, sitting alone at a two-top.

Alone except for Allie, the waitress he was currently berating like she'd run over his dog.

"Can't you get anything right?" He snapped. "You're trash. This whole place is trash. Just shut your mouth and bring me a beer."

Visibly gathering herself, Allie nodded and stepped away. Jim watched as she approached the bar holding a new drink order, her hands trembling.

"Hey, you okay?" he asked softly. "What's going on there?"

"Nothing, it's fine," Allie insisted, sniffling as she squared her shoulders. "One of those tables, you know?"

"Yeah."

Glancing over Allie's shoulder as he poured the man's beer, Jim watched him glare at everything and everyone as if their mere existence offended him. And the more Jim watched, the hotter his blood got. Paying customer or not, no one treated his people like that.

"Come along, Allie," Jim said with a toothy, overcharged smile. "Let's go give excellent customer service to our esteemed patron, shall we?"

Rounding the bar, he took the lead with Allie in tow, and together they delivered the beer.

"Hello, sir," Jim said in a syrupy, conciliatory tone.

"Whatta you want?"

"I was observing your table and, well, I'd like to apologize for the truly terrible service you've received. I was hoping we could make it up to you. Perhaps a free dessert?"

The customer's eyes lit with internal fire. There was someone new to push around, and he was already loving it. "You the manager of this dump?"

"The owner, sir, and it is indeed a dump, I agree. May Allie bring you that dessert now?"

"She'd better. You got two minutes to bring it, or I'm leaving this garbage heap a one-star review."

"Of course, sir, right away." Jim turned to Allie. "Would you bring the gentleman the King's Surprise?"

Allie almost smiled, then schooled her expression. She dipped her head, appearing humbled. "Right away, sir."

As she rushed into the kitchen, Jim gave a parting nod to the customer and returned to his position behind the bar. He grabbed a glass and started polishing while he waited, keeping a lid on his anticipation. Then he noted that Eli was watching him.

He couldn't help grinning. "Ever heard of aspic, Eli?"

Eli shook his head.

"It's an ingredient we save for our most special dessert, for only our most special customers. People whose business really means something."

Allie reemerged from the kitchen, bowl in hand, its contents shiny and red and topped with a crown of whipped cream. Dropping it off with a subservient bow, she scurried behind the bar to stand beside Jim.

"You see, Eli," Jim went on. "The King's Surprise may appear ordinary–just cherry gelatin with fruit and whipped cream–but most people are unaware of aspic, which is the main ingredient."

The bully picked up his spoon and scooped a bite. Allie grabbed Jim's arm in anticipation.

"Allie," Jim said theatrically. "What's aspic?"

"Why, it's just a fancy name for unflavored gelatin, boss."

Jim gave a fake infomercial laugh. "That's right, Allie. And the beauty of aspic? Well, because it's clear and flavorless, you can add whatever you want before the gelatin sets. Like red food dye. And fish broth."

The bully took a bite and instantly gagged. Then his gagging and embarrassment turned to rage. Sweeping the bowl onto the floor with a crash, he stomped over to the bar, where Jim and Allie were falling over each other laughing. The man's face was as red as the gelatin.

"Oh, Gertrude," Jim called. "You're up!"

The customer's hands slapped down on the bar. At the same moment, Jim's favorite bouncer appeared from around the corner. At six-foot-six, with enough muscle to equal Jim's entire body weight, she moved like a brick wall come to life. Jim tossed her an unopened beer can, which she proceeded to crush in her ham-sized fist, spraying foam everywhere.

"What seems to be the problem?" she rumbled.

Staring up at her, the customer seethed but stepped back from the bar, hands up in surrender.

"Now that we're all friends," Jim said sweetly. "Kindly pay for your meal, leave a generous tip, then walk out and never come back. Not until you can behave like all the other nice boys and girls. Deal?"

Somehow the man's scowl deepened as he dug cash out of his wallet and tossed it onto the bar. Without another word, he spun on his heels and stormed out.

"Oh, man, I cannot wait to read his review," Jim said. "Nice work, everyone. This calls for a celebratory high-five."

Gertrude reached across the bar and slapped him five, which felt like slapping a boulder, then returned to her place to keep watch. In truth, she was more bark than bite. Sure, she was a parahuman, so she was way tougher than any regular non-powered person, but her power capacity was only 1.1, which made her a runt in the parahuman world. Still, she was good at her job and all Jim could afford.

Allie hugged his arm. "Thanks, boss. You're a good guy."

Jim feigned outrage. "You take that back. I'm a bad, dangerous man. The sexy kind with a secret heart of gold, and then a smaller, darker heart inside that one."

"Nope, just good," she said, patting him before going back to work.

He smiled, enjoying the afterglow of their little prank. Any night he could serve a literal bowl of instant karma, he counted that as a good one.

"She likes you, you know," Eli said quietly, staring into his glass. "Allie."

"Huh? Nah, no one likes the boss. Bosses are jerks."

No response. Jim glanced at Eli, whose attention was laser-focused on the TV now. Incredibly, Skypuncher was still on camera, only now the shot had widened to reveal all seven of the Spectrum. Wow, they were together for a simple post-world-saving news conference? Usually at least one stayed on the Lighthouse–the orbiting space station that served as their base of operations.

There wasn't anyone on the planet who wouldn't recognize its most revered heroes. It started with the proprietary communicators affixed to each hero's right ear, allowing them to communicate not just verbally but with some level of telepathy.

But they were a minor detail compared to the capes. Each of the seven wore a cape of a different color of the visible light spectrum, all swaying dramatically in the non-existent breeze. No one else in the world wore capes–not even villains–out of respect and deference to the Spectrum. And probably some peer pressure. So the sight of them was always extra dramatic.

"This looks like more than business as usual," Eli said.

"Hey, can you turn that up?" someone called from behind Jim.

He obliged. Then, out of habit, he picked up a tumbler while he watched and busied his hands polishing the glass. No one liked seeing a barman just stand there.

"Lastly, I know there have been whispers, so we've come together to officially confirm the rumors and make the announcement," Skypuncher said. "Ten years ago, we did something unprecedented. We invited a group of up-and-coming heroes to the Lighthouse for what we called the Dare. It was a competition that allowed us to meet and evaluate each of them, and invite the most extraordinary to join the Prisms, our support and response teams. Those who joined us ten years ago have gone on to do incredible things."

Jim tensed. *Not all of them have, and you know it.*

"And yet," Skypuncher continued. "Many have wondered why the Dare only occurred once. Well, in three days–exactly ten years later–that will no longer be the case. The Dare has officially returned!"

Cheers went up from the crowd around the Spectrum. Jim flinched as more cheers rang out across Versus. He hadn't noticed that the whole bar was watching. He was just thankful everyone was looking at his back and couldn't see his face, because it felt like his ribs were constricting around his lungs.

"Invitations are already going out to the next wave of standout heroes. We can't wait to meet you and see what you've got." Skypuncher pointed at the camera. "Soon, *you* just might be one of us."

Something shattered. Jim only half-noticed that he'd dropped the glass.

No no no. Please, not again.

TWO

MEMORIES flooded through Jim's mind, unbidden and unwanted. Dark days that he'd worked very hard to leave behind and never think of again. While his patrons celebrated around him, he moved as if through a fog, going through the motions of managing the bar.

How could the Spectrum do this? Didn't they care how the last Dare had ruined his life? His family? Though he tried maintaining his open, welcoming barman's demeanor, little by little his shock was transmuting into anger.

The last thing he needed was another troublesome customer. So, of course, that's exactly what he got.

The young punk dropped onto a barstool a few seats down from Eli. Slicked-back blonde hair, red velour tracksuit, thick gold chain, gaudy gold watch on the left wrist and a fresh tattoo on the right. It was like he shopped at a store specializing in movie gangster costumes. Something about that tattoo tickled Jim's memory.

He told himself to relax, to make no assumptions. Maybe the guy just wanted a quiet drink in peace. Plastering on a smile, Jim approached.

"Hey, what can I get you?"

"Vodka, rocks," the gangster said in a Russian accent. Because of course he would be Russian and order vodka.

"You got it."

Glass on the bar. Scooped ice. Jim grabbed the vodka on the lowest shelf and upturned it over the glass. As he poured, the gangster leaned closer and spoke so that only Jim would hear.

"I have job for you."

"Is it pouring vodka? Because if so, I'm way ahead of you."

"Special job. Mob-run bank. Front for gambling, money laundering. Very tough security run by artificial intelligence. But if AI servers are cracked . . ." He raised his arms to mime something large. "Big payday, my friend."

Jim's eyebrows lifted. "You want to hire a bartender to crack a bank's security?"

"Not hire bartender. Hire *you*."

"Well, I'm flattered, but I'm also not your guy. I mean, I still play Snake on my phone and it's right in the sweet spot for my computer skills."

"You want more money? We pay more money, is no sweat."

"I'd love more money, so feel free to tip irresponsibly. Aside from that . . ." Jim shrugged.

The gangster scowled, shifting from slimy salesman to slimy enforcer. "You know what I mean, and I know who you are. Who you *really* are."

"Okay okay, you got me," Jim said, feigning regret. "I have overdue library books. I swear, I'll bring them back. I just had to read The Feminine Mystique a third time."

Grinding his teeth, the gangster slapped his phone on the bar and turned on the screen, revealing a grainy photo. Jim went razor straight, all his cheer draining away.

"You are Lock, of old team Lock and Lode. We know this," the gangster said. "Now, my friend, the Chaos Merchant has need of your talents."

The Chaos Merchant—that was the fresh tattoo on his wrist. A gray oval outlined in black, a horizontal black line cutting through the middle, and near the top a smoking bullet hole. The smoke appeared to be in motion, wafting out of the bullet hole like it always did anywhere this symbol appeared. An effect likely achieved by some talented Illusion Controller.

This guy belonged to the last villain that any sane person wanted to cross paths with. Jim swallowed hard. Then, as quickly as it appeared, his fear flashed into rage. He pressed his hands onto the bar and leaned forward.

"First of all, I don't like bullies. Second, you haven't done your research, *friend*. If I even knew who Lock and Lode were, I'd tell you they were aspiring heroes, not thieves. I'd tell you that Lock–the older sibling, *and a girl*–was the Digital Controller and master of computer code. Her brother Lode was an Electric Controller who manipulated stuff that runs on electricity. So if I were Lode, I couldn't hack your bank servers, but I could do this."

Jim snapped his fingers. The gangster's phone engulfed in flames, its battery overloaded.

With a cry, the gangster slapped the phone away. As it tumbled to the floor behind the bar, Jim grabbed his seltzer gun and doused the fire. The expensive-looking device was now a steaming chunk of slag.

"My phone!" the gangster wailed.

"In summation," Jim said, "Even if you had the right guy–which you don't–you still wouldn't have the right guy. Got it?"

The young punk swallowed. "B-but if you cannot do this . . . where do I find Lock?"

Jim's expression darkened. He hooked a thumb over his shoulder, toward Skypuncher's highly punchable face on the TV screen. "Go ask him."

He gave the signal and Gertrude appeared, looming with a smile that said she really enjoyed her job and everything it required. Jim took a deep breath, recovering a sliver of his good nature.

"You're welcome back if you want to drink bad vodka and watch some terrible fights. Until then, it's time to go."

And the gangster did, looking all too happy to put space between himself and Gertrude.

Jim leaned back against the counter behind the bar. Staring into space, he took a series of deep, cleansing breaths to purge what had just happened. He didn't like going to that dark place. Much better to serve up drinks and smiles.

When he came back to the present, restored to his usual self, he noted Eli eyeing him between sips.

"My one regret," Jim said. "Is that I didn't offer him a free dessert."

For the first time since he sat down, Eli laughed out loud.

Jim grinned. "I'm running a flash sale. Anyone who didn't see what just happened gets another round of my best scotch, on the house."

Eli slid his glass forward. "Deal."

Jim passed one last sweeping glance over Versus, now dark and quiet. Everything seemed to be in its place, so he set the alarm and stepped outside, locking the door behind him.

The service door opened onto an empty alley. This part of Highreach had seen less and less use over the decades, with fewer people finding reason to venture here. At this point, the converted old brick warehouse that held Versus and Jim's loft apartment was surrounded mostly by other warehouses. Still, the commute was blissfully short and undisturbed by people.

At the alley mouth, Jim turned left on Morrison Street, his gaze sweeping over the city as he walked. The whole thing was divided into districts, each named after an old hero, and this one was called Thunderous.

It was darker and quieter here at 3 a.m. But the busier districts, like Eightball and Halcyon? They still bustled, bright and modern lights throwing the old architecture into stark relief. Deep shadows were cast by angular stone buildings, gothic spires and half-eroded statues, which contrasted with the slightly newer (but still old) industrial complexes that had sprung up between them over decades.

The only shiny new thing in Highreach was the skyscraper for Atherton Industries, which Jim could see the top half of from where he stood. He liked the place without knowing why. Maybe he found it funny how out-of-place it was, with its curving lines of glass and steel and sparkling white stone, reaching far above everything else. It looked like it belonged in Cloudreach, but some giant had plucked it from there and dropped it in the middle of Highreach instead, as some grand practical joke.

At that thought, Jim peered in the other direction and up, toward Cloudreach–Highreach's twin city in name only. Massive, modern, sparkling and beautiful, it was the belle of the ball while Highreach was the janitor that swept up afterward.

Highreach had come first, founded over two hundred years ago on the shorter of two gigantic rocky plateaus rising from a vast desert. Over decades it had slowly grown into a prosperous city. Until ninety years ago, when Highreach's water leasing deals were approaching renewal. A desert city, it had to pipe in all its fresh water from other regions, and those contracts were vital to keeping the pipes flowing.

Water was expensive, and bringing it here even more-so. Which is why the richest tycoons in Highreach decided to pack up and move to the taller plateau, where they founded Cloudreach. Their first move had been to take control of the water contracts and build new pipes that fed Cloudreach first and Highreach second, ensuring that all new money and business would flow through their city first.

Needless to say, there was a rivalry to this day, which Jim happily participated in. Maybe that was why he liked having the Atherton building right where it was.

It might also have been the amount of power that ran it, which was insane. Jim could see–and feel–electricity coursing through Highreach in a pulsing web, everything from thick transfer cables carrying heavy loads for factories to tiny threads feeding individual homes. The lifeblood of the city. The sense had been part of him since childhood, when his power had manifested, so at this point he barely thought about it. It was kind of like seeing a color that other people couldn't.

But Atherton glowed like a warm beacon. Jim could point to the building even with his eyes closed. He had no idea what they did in there, but he could almost feel the charge on his skin even from miles away.

As he turned off Morrison and headed down the next alley, an electrical tremor passed through him. Atherton must be working extra hard tonight.

Wait. That wasn't from Atherton. Jim stopped and turned in a circle, staring into the shadows. Something heavily electrical brushed his perception, yet all was silent and still.

"If something out there is waiting to rob me," Jim called. "You should know that I'm not afraid to scream like a child."

Nothing. Shrugging, he walked to another nondescript door, nearly identical to the service entrance for Versus. One advantage to his home looking like a rundown warehouse–no one thought there was anything inside worth stealing.

Jim pulled out his keys . . . and froze. There it was, that electrical presence, and it was getting closer.

His powers went active now. He stretched out his senses, seeking instead of just receiving. The large presence split and resolved into four smaller signatures. They were surrounding him, two coming from his left while two approached from the shadows to his right. Their power cores were tiny, but now Jim could see pinpricks of blue-white energy.

Pocketing his keys, he suppressed a wave of fear. His last real fight had been at eighteen, ten years ago now. He tried not to imagine how badly this could go.

They were close now. Close enough to give off a faint mechanical whirring. Was this related to that gangster who tried to hire him? Maybe the Chaos Merchant didn't take no for an answer.

Well, no sense waiting to be cut down in an alley. He might as well go down like a child throwing a tantrum. Tensing, he raised fists and spun.

He burst out laughing with relief and leaned back against his door. "You really know how to spook a guy. Is that in your programming?"

Four OmniBots floated in a half circle around him. The machines were shaped like giant bullets standing on their flat end, about five feet tall. Cylindrical bodies, conical heads, a metal exterior crisscrossed with overlapping lines where doors could pop open for all manner of tools and appendages. The front half of each head was a screen projecting cartoon faces and expressions. Right now they were smiling and emitting friendly little beeps.

OmniBots had no weapons, only tools. The Spectrum used them as service and maintenance crew on the Lighthouse, and occasionally as messengers.

Actually, now that Jim thought about it, *only* the Spectrum used them. He sobered and stood straight. Why were they here? It couldn't be connected with that announcement tonight, could it? There's no way they would invite Jim. Not after his last conversation with Skypuncher ten years ago.

A conversation that had ended with Jim's hand broken and Skypuncher's chin scorched by an electrical burn.

But why else would they be here? Attempting to be gracious, Jim prepared his most eloquent rejection. "Hey, look, I know it's been a long time and you may think it's all water under the bridge. But I should tell you–"

A harsh warning buzz replaced the OmniBots' pleasant beeps. Their cartoon smiles switched to angry frowny faces. A door popped open on the left-most machine, revealing a cutting torch.

Before Jim could ask what it was for, flames shot at his face.

THREE

JIM dropped to the ground. Fire filled the air where his head had been. His front door scorched, cheap paint bubbling under intense heat.

The other OmniBots tracked his movement, extending deadly tools of their own. Jim glimpsed a saw blade and a laser cutter before rolling away. Flying saw blades chewed into the pavement where he'd been.

He came to his feet facing the wrong direction, his back exposed to the machines. There wasn't even time to be afraid before he felt a swell of electrical power. One of the OmniBots was powering up for a bigger attack. Dodging aside, Jim flowed into a cartwheel and immediately tumbled in a heap with a heavy *oof*. It had been at least a decade since he'd tried that move. Come to think of it, he'd fallen that time, too.

A bright red laser sliced through the air where he'd been standing. The terrible cartwheel had been enough to save his life.

He climbed to his feet, then noticed his shirt was on fire.

With a yelp, Jim stopped-dropped-and-rolled, which ironically saved him again as a projectile flew overhead and disappeared into the shadows. He ripped off the flaming shirt and tossed it away just as a garbage bin exploded.

"This is a messed up way to say you're sorry!" he said, wincing at the scorch mark on his shoulder.

All four OmniBots reoriented on Jim, targeting beams clustered on his chest. He felt his guts drop to his feet. Clumsy dodges weren't going to save him this time.

Eyes wide, screaming like something angry and tough and definitely *not* like a frightened child, Jim charged. This seemed to catch the machines by surprise, since they didn't instantly cut him to pieces, giving him barely enough time to dive and somersault across the ground.

"WHY AM I DOING THIS?" he shouted.

Rolling close enough to the laser cutter OmniBot, he slapped his hands against the shell. His senses burst with static.

Thirteen Years Ago

"Okay, Jimmy," Summer said. "It's for real this time. Just stick with the plan and we'll be fine. Right?"

"Um, yeah." Jimmy's voice cracked. He paused and tried again, making his voice deeper. "Yes. It's what we've been training for."

"And they'll never know what hit 'em."

Jimmy eyed his older sister, trying not to look scared. She wore an eager grin, as if she couldn't wait to begin. They crouched together on a rooftop in the Redgate district of Highreach. Beneath their feet, the Twisted Pair gang hid in their lair after another robbery. Their *last* robbery, if all went well tonight.

Summer reached over to adjust his mask, and then straightened her own. Suddenly self-conscious, Jimmy tugged at his costume. It had that feeling of new clothes that hadn't conformed to his shape yet. Which made sense, since this was the first time he'd worn it.

He shivered and told himself it was from the chill. This damp, misty night was uncommon for a desert city. He could smell the dust kicked up by the raindrops.

Blowing out a quick breath, he squared his shoulders. It was time to focus.

It was time to be a hero.

"I'm ready," he said.

Summer nodded. "It's go time."

She pressed both hands against a thick bundle of wires that ran along the rooftop. Jimmy mirrored her, palms against his own target–a thick metal pipe. As he made firm contact, his senses came alive. A wave of exhilaration swept through him. It was like he could feel the building's heartbeat, follow the pulses into every corner. He felt all the flows of electricity, saw them in his mind, a web of power that was now his to command.

Now for his best trick–the thing Summer had made him swear never to tell anyone he could do. Though he still didn't understand why. As if he were breathing in, he pulled on that electric web and drew some of its power into his body. It felt like absorbing fireworks into his bloodstream.

As he drank it in, his range of perception expanded. His grip on the electricity around him strengthened, as did his focus and control. Not only could he touch that web of power, he could do the same with everything connected to it. Anything in the building that ran on electricity was now subject to his will.

The look on Summer's face told him she was feeling it, too, in a different way. With hands wrapped around the data cables feeding to and from the building, she could perceive the streams of computer code like he could feel the flows of electricity. As his grip tightened around everything that ran on electricity, hers took control of anything with even a simple computer, anything that relied on code to function.

They looked at each other. With a glint in her eye, Summer tensed.

Every phone, computer, and security camera in the building scrambled. Though he couldn't sense the code, Jimmy felt the effect of her commands on the flow of electricity, and knew it was his turn now.

He flexed that electricity running through the building as if it were an extension of his muscles. Overhead lights sparked and burst. Phone batteries overloaded. The gang was plunged into darkness and confusion. Jimmy told the doors' electronic locks to open.

Summer released her cables and Jimmy released his pipe. They dashed to the edge of the roof and looked over the side, grappling hooks in hand.

"Ready to take down our first gang?" Summer said, bursting with glee.

Flying high on power, Jimmy raised his fist. "For Highreach."

Summer bumped his fist with hers. "Always."

With a cry, they leapt over the edge.

Hands on the OmniBot, Jim gasped. Long-ignored sensations roared to life. He hadn't done anything like this for a decade. He'd purposely avoided it.

But now, as he connected with the electrical flow inside the machine, as his mind perceived its inner workings, old, neglected instincts came back with them. He remembered exactly what to do.

So he aimed the OmniBot at its fellow machines and gave it a single, overriding command.

Kill.

Jim crouched as mayhem erupted overhead, lasers and flames and spinning blades and explodey things flying back and forth, the other three OmniBots now forced to defend themselves against one of their own. Jim kept a tight grip on his pet machine, mentally shouting his command over and over.

It only took seconds. Then the cacophony of battle ceased, replaced by the clanging symphony of demolished machines toppling to the pavement. Only his pet OmniBot remained somewhat upright, and it wouldn't attack him now anyway. He stood, feeling something he'd long since forgotten–the thrill of surviving what should have killed him.

Whooping, Jim grabbed what was left of his OmniBot and kissed the back of its scorched conical head. "Oh, you beautiful murderbot."

The head swiveled, pointing the screen at him, and its cartoon expression was replaced by a real person. A face hidden behind a helmet and mask.

"Gah!" Jim stumbled back.

"Don't run, James Riven," the face said. "I'm a friend."

"You make friends by sending machines to kill them? If you want to be *best* friends, why not burn down my bar, too?"

"Look," the face said. "Listen."

The OmniBot couldn't hurt him now, Jim knew that much. As the initial shock faded, he actually looked at the image on the screen. Dark gray helmet and flat, featureless faceplate, only broken by a narrow eye slit that glowed with internal purple light. But the eyes looking out through it were a real person's.

Jim replayed the voice in his head, paying attention to the deep and echoing sound. It called to mind the image of a barrel-chested old scholar making grand proclamations from the dais of an ancient library.

Jim's eyes widened. "Lord Neon."

"Correct."

He was standing face to face–well, sort of–with one of the Spectrum. The weirdest, most mysterious one of all. No one had ever defined what his powers really were. Lord Neon just *knew* things that no one else knew, or could know.

"I didn't send the OmniBots," Lord Neon said. "Someone else must have discovered the truth and taken steps to keep it from you."

"What truth? I've been nobody for ten years, and I've done that on purpose. There's no information worth killing me over."

"The truth about your sister. That she is still alive."

What? Jim's heart lurched and raced and stumbled all at once. He broke into a cold sweat, more disturbed than when the machines were trying to kill him.

"I thought she was classified Missing, Presumed Dead. Was that a lie?"

"Not a lie. A shield. Not all misinformation is meant to harm, James. Sometimes it is meant to protect."

Working to hide the storm of emotions, Jim furrowed his brow. "I don't get it. First, Skypuncher tells me Summer probably died in action. Now, years later, you're telling me she might actually be alive. Which is it, and why tell me now?"

"Summer Riven, known by the world as Lock, disappeared and likely perished in battle with the villain Framework," Lord Neon explained. "That is the official story, as you were told, and it will remain so. But it is not the whole truth. The complete record was carefully concealed on the Lighthouse, in a place known only to a few. I believe that concealment has been compromised. This knowledge is far more dangerous than you can imagine, Jim. So, now we must face that danger head-on, together."

The longer Lord Neon spoke, the more control Jim was able to regain over his roiling insides, slowly becoming himself again. As he came back together, he recalled a truth that he'd realized on the day Skypuncher knocked on his door with news that Summer was dead. A truth that dragged old, buried anger to the surface.

"If the Spectrum's lied to me before, you could be lying now," he said. "You may be the world's greatest heroes, but I don't trust any of you as far as I can kick you. You say there's danger? Deal with it yourself. I'm a bartender."

"James, you must listen. There is more to–"

Jim sent a final command to the OmniBot. With a false grin, he waved at the screen.

"Bye-bye, now."

The OmniBot deployed its laser cutter and turned the weapon on itself. In a blaze of light, it clattered to the ground in smoking pieces.

Turning his back on the wreckage, Jim opened his blistered front door and stepped inside. Tonight was an anomaly, he told himself. The exact kind of night he had constructed this life to avoid. Nothing was going to disturb that.

"Honey, I'm home," he called to the empty air.

He felt the pleasant, familiar spark-zing of connecting with the power grid running his home–built from reclaimed brick and ancient steel, which he'd converted to a large loft apartment. At his will, the lights and TV and game console switched on. As he strolled to the living room and plopped down on the worn leather couch, he also willed the blast chiller to ice down a beer.

Cake. He wanted cake. Maybe later he would bake a cake with pineapple in it. That always soothed him. Wait, why was he cold? Oh, right, the murderbots had set his shirt on fire. He snatched an old Whiplash Smile t-shirt from their final tour off the back of his aviator chair and slipped it over his head.

Controller in hand, he was preparing to launch a game when movement caught his eye from a place where there should be no movement. He dropped the controller and whirled to his feet, facing the wall of glass that led to the rooftop terrace. The only way to get out there was through the loft, and hardly anyone ever came into his loft. Yet, there stood a figure, peering at him through the glass.

For a long moment, they stared at each other. Jim mentally dared the figure to make a move, but he knew that wasn't going to happen. This visitor would not enter uninvited, but he also wouldn't leave until they had whatever conversation he came here to have. Sighing, Jim flicked his finger and the wide stretch of glass slid smoothly into the wall.

The visitor stepped inside, hands behind his back beneath the violet cape. He stood nearly seven feet tall and wore dark gray armor, blocky and heavy-looking like stone, yet his movements rippled like a panther. The glowing eye slit in that flat gray faceplate mirrored the thin line of purple light across his chest.

Jim narrowed his eyes. "What do you really want?"

"To reveal the truth about Summer," Lord Neon said, deep voice echoing as if he were addressing a reverent audience in some grand stone chamber. "And to help you find her."

FOUR

"**THANKS** for helping out back there," Jim said sardonically.

"I discovered what was happening too late to divert the OmniBots without attracting attention," Lord Neon explained. "Though observing the battle did confirm beyond doubt who you are."

"It's not like I changed my name or anything."

"I was referring to your other identity. Lode, and his instincts, are still inside you, even if you ignore them. My agent also confirms this."

"Agent?"

"You met him earlier this evening."

Then it dawned on Jim. "The Russian gangster. That's why the Chaos Merchant tattoo looked so new. Because it was fake."

"Correct."

"You know, you could have just asked me."

"Because you would have been willing to talk?"

Jim considered, then inclined his head. "Okay, good point. You're here now, so speak your piece. Then I have a date with a pineapple cake."

"I do not believe the timing of this attack is coincidence. Lock was our most promising recruit from the original Dare.

Now, ten years later and on the eve of the next Dare, someone finds her brother and tries to kill him."

"If they thought I would try out, they're morons."

"More likely, they do not want to risk that you will learn the truth, even by accident. Logically, that means I must help you."

"Help me find the truth about Summer, or track down whoever sent the machines?"

"I believe one will lead to the other. The closer you draw to Lock, the more it may force your aggressor into the open, where we can confront him."

"So, you want me to be your chum," Jim said. "Not *friend* chum. *Dropped in the water with sharks* chum. And for what? Some file about my sister with a forwarding address? Let me guess–she has six kids and drives a truck in Wichita?"

Lord Neon stared hard at him for a long moment. Too long a moment. *Way* too long a moment, and it was getting awkward. He wasn't moving a muscle.

Puzzled, Jim cocked his head and leaned closer. "Uh, anyone home?" He waved hands in front of the hero's blank, motionless eyes. "Hello? Oil can?"

Lord Neon suddenly twitched. With a heavy grunt, as if it took all his strength to move, he reached up to the Spectrum communicator affixed to his head. He pressed it and appeared to listen to something. Then, as if nothing at all had happened, he resumed speaking.

"There is risk to this plan, of course."

"Dude."

"But ours is a life of risk."

"No, yours is a life of risk. Mine is a life of beer. And what was that just now? Did you have some kind of glitch?"

"What was what?"

"Ugh. Never mind. Not like it changes my answer."

"Which is?"

"I think you already know."

Lord Neon studied Jim before he answered. "I don't know you well, James, but I do know how much Summer meant to you. The young man I saw ten years ago would have done anything on Earth for a chance like this. Even if it meant facing danger. Even if it meant getting involved with heroes."

Jim wanted so badly to tell this man how wrong he was. He tried to say the words, tried to be dismissive and unaffected. But a lie that big wouldn't come out of his mouth. Not when it came to Summer.

His head drooped. "Tell me your plan. I'm not saying I'll do it, but . . . just tell me."

"As we speak, I am accessing all information about James Riven in the Lighthouse database, and concealing it. It will be replaced with a new file on James Cranston, a low-level hero wannabe who can switch anything that runs on electricity on or off at will. A harmless but occasionally useful power that has prompted him to adopt the hero moniker Interruptor."

"Well, he sounds delightful. What is he supposed to do?"

"His name has been added to the list of those invited for the Dare."

"What?!"

"In three days, when you go to the Lighthouse to compete as Jim Cranston, you will use the opportunity to secretly track down the information you need."

"I don't want to be part of your little Willy Wonka fantasy."

"Even now, the truth about Summer–what happened to her, where she has been all this time–is hidden somewhere on the Lighthouse. Would you really choose to leave it there? Hasn't this been what you desired for a decade?"

Jim huffed, feeling constricted. "Why do you even care if I find it? You're supposed to know everything, so obviously you already know where it is and what it says. Why not just tell me? Why send me on some chase? And why is the truth suddenly so dangerous?"

Lord Neon simply looked at him.

"Of course." Jim tossed up his hands. "You're an enigma wrapped in a mystery, with a chewy nougat center. No one ever knows what you know, or why you do what you do. Right? That's your brand, isn't it?"

Again, Lord Neon peered at him calmly. Waiting.

"I left that life years ago!" Jim insisted, pointing at the hero in accusation. "I did it on purpose, and I've never regretted it."

"But is that really true?"

That simple question stopped Jim in his tracks.

"Stasis equals death," Lord Neon continued. "It is already apparent that your alternate life plan is not working. You hide from the world in a Warded Zone, running a bar that declines year by year until it will eventually crumble, allowing no one to get close. You, and this life you have constructed around yourself, are slowly and inevitably imploding." He stepped closer, leaning toward Jim as if subtly imploring him. "The answer is out there. *She* is out there. But to discover the truth, you'll have to leave this decaying cocoon and take a risk. You only have to remember who you were, and take the first step."

Jim leaned away from Lord Neon, not wanting to admit how the words drilled him right between the eyes. No one spoke to him like that anymore. Because he hadn't let anyone come close enough to do it. The real truth? The last person who really saw who he was had been Summer.

Suddenly, he had to know. When he spoke again, his voice was hoarse with desperation. "Have . . . have you seen her?"

"No."

Jim's shoulders sagged.

"But perhaps *you* will. Soon."

Lord Neon stepped back. Before leaving, he gestured to the coffee table, where a sealed box waited. How had that gotten there?

"Should you decide that Summer is worth the risk, open the box."

Before turning away, he paused and fixed his eye on Jim. "I have always wanted to ask. Why did Lode stop fighting evil after Lock was gone? Why turn away from a hero's life when you both loved it so much?"

Jim donned a careless grin. "Well, I'd been outgrowing the costume for a while, and the fabric chafed something awful in the crotch area. No one talks about that part of being a hero. You know?"

Lord Neon's voice grew quieter. "Did you really hate us so much?"

Jim's fake smile faltered. He cleared his throat. "I, um, tried to keep going, actually. But the truth is, without Summer, it just wasn't the same. I still wanted to make it work, but then your battle with Framework happened, and then Skypuncher showed up at my door." He looked down at the floor. "After that, I . . . didn't have it in me."

He had never admitted that to anyone. Now that the words were out there, the weight of them threatened to pull him through the floor. He waited, sagging and exhausted, for Lord Neon to judge him for his weakness.

"I understand," the hero said. "More than you know."

Jim looked up at that. To his shock, he saw compassion in the larger-than-life hero's eyes. Lord Neon almost seemed to hesitate.

"I hope, James Riven, that you find what you seek. And that our paths cross again."

He turned, and then he was gone. He left Jim alone, in silence, next to a box that seemed to fill up the room with its presence.

FIVE

JIM didn't sleep that night. He barely even sat down. When morning came, he left Versus in the manager's hands, and set out. While his body walked the streets of Highreach, his mind flipped and spun and tried to process what was happening.

Summer . . .

Lord Neon had been right, as much as Jim hated to admit it. This life he had built–it connected directly back to Summer. Never knowing exactly how she'd died, and watching as those questions slowly destroyed his family. Now he lived inside a shield so the world could not find him or touch him.

Except, now it seemed there was more to the story. If he wanted to find the answers, he'd have to step outside the walls he'd built because of the questions.

The city streamed by like a fog, random landmarks resolving into reality as they connected with Jim's long-buried memories. He passed by Donuts at Dawn, in the Freefall district–his and Summer's favorite breakfast spot. Sometimes as kids they would sneak there instead of going to their first classes. They served a buttermilk pastry with enough calories to last a week, so of course that's what Summer ordered every time. They were training hard and would work off the calories, she had insisted. Now, even from across the street, he could smell them baking.

Two blocks down was the ramshackle building where, at thirteen and sixteen years old, Lock and Lode had taken down a street-level gang whose idea of a good time was assaulting the old and the weak for the cash in their wallets. As they had watched from a rooftop while the gang was handcuffed and loaded into a police transport, Jim had known he'd found his purpose. He wanted to do this every day for the rest of his life.

Four years later, their dad had opened the front door to reveal Skypuncher. The world's greatest hero had come personally to invite Summer for something new they were trying. Tentatively, they were calling it the Dare. She had beamed for days, overflowing with joy and anticipation as she packed a bag and left for the Lighthouse. It was all happening like they'd dreamed.

A few months later, there had been another knock, and once again Skypuncher stood there filling up their doorway with his massive frame. Only this time he wasn't smiling. This time he was hunched, face drawn and haggard as if he carried the weight of a planet on his shoulders.

He didn't have to say anything. After watching on the news what Framework had done to downtown Sydney, hearing rumors about what that victory had cost the Spectrum and their Prism support teams, Jim's mother took one look at Skypuncher's face and collapsed in the foyer, sobbing and screaming her daughter's name.

Had Skypuncher lied to them? If so, why? If Summer might actually be alive, why was she hiding even from her own family? Why was someone so committed to Jim not finding the answers, and why attack him now? Why had Lord Neon said the truth about Summer was dangerous? There were too many questions, and that didn't count the biggest one Jim faced.

Was he going to accept Lord Neon's offer–his challenge, really–to find out?

At that, Jim stopped. The fog around him dissipated enough to reveal how far he'd gone. Moving on autopilot, he must have hopped a train at some point, because he wasn't even in Highreach anymore. He'd ascended to Cloudreach, and stood now at Summer's favorite lookout.

The twin cities couldn't have been more different–one a dark stone relic punctuated by industry, the other a sparkling work of art with crystalline spires. As if modern-day fantasy elves had built a city specifically to look down on the neighboring dwarves.

Summer had never cared about the rivalry, which was why this spot had been her favorite. From here, you could see the best parts of both cities at once. More than anyone else Jim knew, she had seen the beauty in both.

Ten Years Ago

"You turn eighteen in a few days, right?" Summer said.

Jim nodded. "Yep."

"Pick a day job yet?"

"Not one that'll pay for a costume *that* fancy."

He gestured at her brand new costume–the one the Spectrum had fabricated for her. It made their old homemade costumes look like bargain basement cosplay.

Summer blushed, glancing down at herself. The material was electric blue with silver thread in geometric patterns, making her almost look like an armored circuit board. She had peeled away from her Prism after a training mission, and only had enough time for a quick dinner with the family. Which meant she'd had to stay in costume, and now the Rivens had the newest world-class hero sitting in their backyard. She had conceded to taking off the mask, though.

"I've gotta admit, it's hard not to feel like a hero wearing this." She gave Jim a significant look. "Which reminds me, you should know I'll be putting your name out there soon. With your record, you're already on the Spectrum's radar, but a little extra push never hurt anyone." She raised an eyebrow. "You can finally meet Geometron."

Now it was Jim's turn to blush. Geometron wore the orange cape. She was half human, half cyborg, all ridiculously hot, and she'd been Jim's hero crush for years.

"How many times do you think I'll have to save the world before she notices me?"

"Oh, at least three."

"Figures. I don't suppose you'd want to pretend to threaten the world so I can pretend to take you down. That's gotta earn me at least a phone number, right?"

Summer laughed. "Don't worry. Sooner or later, we'll save the world together. It's just a matter of time."

The memory faded, leaving Jim alone on the lookout. As it turned out, that was their last happy memory together. A week later, Framework appeared in Australia and wreaked enough havoc for the Spectrum to rush in and help the overwhelmed local heroes.

It had started with a strange wave of cold that emanated from Hyde Park, covering half the city in a layer of frost. Then, as the battle raged on, Framework had caused entire blocks to come alive like a living organism, and was laying waste to everything when the Spectrum arrived. It took almost two full days of constant battle, and the lives of far too many heroes–even a few sympathetic villains–before Framework finally fell.

Three days later, Skypuncher had knocked on their door.

Jim gazed out over the Reaches and let it all wash over him again. The confusion, the gaping loss, the anger, and finally the questions. The questions were all they had left of Summer.

Thinking back to his teenage self, Jim knew exactly what he would have done to get answers.

And if there had been even a sliver of a chance that those answers might lead to Summer, would anything on this planet have stopped him?

Jim sprinted away from the lookout and called up Chariot, the rideshare app. He grabbed a ride back to Highreach, to Morrison Street and his loft behind Versus. He threw open the door and tore up the stairs as if he were on fire and the only extinguisher lay in a box on his coffee table.

I'm only going to find answers about Summer, he promised himself. *If Lord Neon has some plan to draw me back into his world, he'll be disappointed. Once I find Summer, I'm coming right back here to Versus and never even thinking the word* hero *again.*

Skidding to a stop, he stared down at the box left by Lord Neon. After racing all this way, now he hesitated.

"Come on, idiot, stop pretending," he said to himself. "The second he left this here, you knew what you were going to do."

Still, it took all his strength to reach out. Hands shaking, he traced fingertips tentatively across the top of the box.

Something inside beeped. With an electric hum, the top slid open.

Jim stared at the contents. "He has got to be kidding."

SIX

CLOUDREACH was a ridiculous place. The buildings were too shiny, the air was too clean, and somehow the whole city smelled like fresh cinnamon rolls. People on the street smiled at you, and they didn't even try to steal your wallet after.

Still, Jim didn't have much choice about being here. Today he was catching a ride to the Lighthouse, and the coordinates Lord Neon had given him were right smack in the middle of Grinningmoronville.

The train dropped him at the Innovation district. Cloudreach named all their districts after . . . aspirational ideals. Ugh. Gag. Instead of naming stuff after heroes like normal people, these jabronis had to get all superior. They named their districts things like Endeavor, Tenacity, Splendor, and one was actually called Aspiration. Jim didn't know if you could punch a city in the face, but he was willing to try.

Careful to avoid strolling so that no one would think he enjoyed it here, Jim stomped down several city blocks. He came to Meltzer Park and stomped across the central green expanse. On the far side, he stomped into a thick copse of trees.

Most of the junk that Lord Neon had put in the mystery box was now in a backpack slung over Jim's shoulder. Fake credentials, a phone to go with his alias, and a ridiculous costume that he wouldn't wear even if it kept the fresh-baked stench of Cloudreach off him. Jeans, flannel button-up in muted blue, and his favorite work boots–those were his hero costume now. Never again would he wear something clingy in a primary color, even if . . .

Wait. Directly ahead, electricity flowed in a circular pattern. In a forest in the middle of a park. Whatever he'd stumbled across, it was so heavily shielded that even Jim hadn't sniffed it out until he was right on top of it. He pushed his senses out and the blue-white streams of energy came into focus.

It wasn't a weapon. He could tell that much by how the power was being consumed. Which, combined with knowing that the Spectrum was running this show, left one likely explanation.

Jim stepped forward.

Whoa.

He'd been expecting it, but the effect was still disorienting. Looking ahead, the thick trees had seemed to stretch on for another few hundred meters. Yet, between one step and the next, the forest disappeared to reveal a circular clearing about a hundred feet across.

Holograms. They're projecting a forest over this clearing to hide their pickup point.

As if that weren't pretentious enough, now the air smelled like an enchanted fairy tale forest *and* cinnamon rolls.

"Seriously, what a trash fire," Jim muttered.

He wasn't the only one here. On opposite sides of the clearing, there were two smaller circles outlined in the grass. Six people stood in the nearest circle, all fresh-faced and eager to prove themselves. Jim didn't want to get any of their enthusiasm on him, so he angled across the clearing, where only one person occupied that circle.

He felt a flash of anxiety. This was it. Starting now, the game was on. Time to put that new identity to the test.

Stepping inside the circle, he faced the other man. Tall and broad-shouldered, with floppy dark hair and thick-framed glasses, he turned to Jim with a big, welcoming smile.

"Hey." Jim offered his hand. "I'm Jim Cran–"

"Jim Riven! How the heck are ya, man? It's been like fifteen years." The man grabbed his hand and pumped it like they were long-lost buddies.

Oh, come on! Four seconds in, and my cover's already blown?

For a split second, Jim considered that maybe he sucked as much as Cloudreach did.

No. That was impossible.

But it was close.

"Um," Jim said, at a total loss for how to recover. Staring up at this stranger in wide-eyed shock, he realized something. This *wasn't* a stranger. He just had a better memory than Jim. "Hold on. Kelvin . . . Haskel?"

"Yeah, man. Sixth grade, Mrs. Syken's class. That lady was a real hoot, let me tell you. Did you stick around here after that? My family moved to Wisconsin before seventh grade."

"Highreach, born and raised."

"Right on, that's super swell. Hey, are we still shaking hands?"

Jim looked down at their hands, still clasped and moving up and down. "It would appear that we are."

"I thought so. Shall we stop, old buddy?"

"You got it, friend."

They released grips. Wow, Kelvin was sporting some high-end battery powered implants–Jim had felt the current as they shook hands. He'd seen this before, with people who'd been in serious accidents and had some of their insides rebuilt. There was probably a sad story there, so he'd make sure not to ask. Instead, he wracked his brain for a way to ask an old childhood friend to call him a fake name without making it weird.

Kelvin leaned closer and lowered his voice. "Hey, before anyone else gets here, can I ask a favor?"

"Only if I can ask one back."

"Oh, I insist," Kelvin said. Clearly, they were both going to ignore how awkwardly polite they were being. "Anyway, this may seem weird, but I'm going by Kelvin Scott now. It's a long story, but I might have made some dubious decisions as a youth and then gotten some help to reinvent myself. I've been building low-level hero cred with this new identity."

Well, this couldn't be more perfect.

"Say no more, old friend," Jim said magnanimously. "You want to be Kelvin Scott, you got it. And while we're on the subject, would you mind terribly calling me Jim Cranston?"

"Absolutely. Hey, we'll be alias buddies. Are you escaping a criminal record, too?"

"Uh, no, I'm in . . . uh, witness protection."

NO, YOU IDIOT.

Kelvin's eyebrows raised. "Really? Wow, they only changed your last name, and they didn't make you move away?"

"Um."

You're stuck with it now. Idiot.

Jim forced a chuckle. "Yeah, the Marshalls on my case are super lazy. I've almost been assassinated like a dozen times."

"Wow." Kelvin slapped him on the shoulder. "Well, no worries, buddy. Your secret's safe with me."

"Appreciate that," Jim said, blown away that it had actually worked.

Covertly eyeing his new old friend, he couldn't help wondering if Kelvin Haskel-now-Scott was another one of Lord Neon's projects. It would be like that guy to have more than one scheme going on during the Dare. In fact, the more Jim considered it, the more likely it seemed.

"Looks like we'll have company." Kelvin nodded over Jim's shoulder. "Don't worry, I don't recognize either of them from middle school."

Jim turned to see two women crossing the clearing. The first was an Asian woman with a pixie cut, five feet tall at most. With a beaming face and eager eyes, she bounced when she stepped, as if she still had hope for a bright future. Having hope meant she couldn't be more than nineteen or twenty.

The second woman . . .

Jim nearly stopped breathing. The second woman was going to be his kryptonite. He knew it down to his bones. Petite yet curvy. Long chestnut hair and dark, smoky eyes. A smile that lit up her whole face and made those dark eyes twinkle. If Jim were a poet . . . well, he wouldn't start spouting poetry at her, because that would be creepy and probably ruin his chances right away. But he would be tempted.

They arrived before he fully recovered his wits. Fortunately, Pixie Cut bought him time. Stepping forward, she grabbed and vigorously shook both his and Kelvin's hands at the same time.

"Hi, I'm Natalie Yu! I'm so thrilled to be here with you and see the Lighthouse and meet all my heroes and audition for a Prism. It's so exciting! Are you guys super excited?"

Jim didn't think he'd ever been that excited about anything. "Oh yeah. I hear the Lighthouse cafeteria serves a mean chowder."

"Really? Awesome!" Natalie rolled on, unfazed. "Who are you guys hoping to meet? My favorite is Millennia. I cannot wait to see her in person."

Millennia, who wore the green cape, was a warrior princess born into the Shang Dynasty during China's Bronze Age. Ageless, incredibly tough, and enigmatic in a completely different way than someone like Lord Neon. Some theorized that she may have been the very first parahuman.

"What a great day. I already made a new friend." Natalie glanced at the other woman, then at the two men. "*Three* friends, and we're all here to stand against evil."

"Right on. Up top." Kelvin held up a hand for her to slap five, which she did. "Hey, I'm Kelvin and this is Jim. Let's hope evil has a comfortable chair ready, because we're going to make it sit down."

"Can I bring a chair, too?" Jim asked. "I'm totally ready to sit against evil."

He aimed his grin at the dark-eyed woman, whose brow furrowed.

"Can I help you with something?" she said.

Only then did Jim realize he'd been looking at her the entire time since they'd stepped into the circle.

Great job, James. Really smooth.

Hey, I warned you, James. Kryptonite.

Natalie put a hand on her new friend's shoulder. "Guys, this is Zoe Blake."

"Hey." Zoe nodded but didn't offer a hand.

Her eyes kept moving, as if she were constantly noticing everyone and everything around her. Jim could practically see the wheels turning inside her head. He wanted to ask what her powers were, but held back. When he'd been active, it was considered rude to ask about someone's powers unless they volunteered it first.

Natalie had no such reservations. "Hey, what's everyone's power class? What's your moniker? Tell me everything!"

Despite his cold, black heart, Jim couldn't help enjoying the little whirlwind of joy that was Natalie Yu. She'd probably spend the first hour on the Lighthouse collecting selfies and autographs from all the heroes.

Kelvin cleared his throat. "Um, well, they call me Delete. I'm a Light Controller, and I do this." He pointed at Natalie's wristwatch, which shimmered and disappeared. "If I focus on something, I can make it so the light doesn't touch it."

"That's the coolest thing ever!" Natalie squealed. "Jim?"

"Ah," Jim said. "They call me Captain Flannel."

Natalie's smile turned disbelieving. "I don't think flannel is a power."

"Well, clearly you don't know how much static I can generate like *this*."

Jim swiped his palms vigorously up and down his torso, rubbing against the flannel shirt. Then he reached up and touched the tip of Kelvin's nose.

Zap

"Ow," Kelvin said.

"Ta-da!" Jim raised his arms theatrically.

"Okay then," Natalie said, still smiling but unsure.

Jim noted a private little smirk on Zoe's face. Did she think he was funny, or an idiot? Probably somewhere in the middle. That was his sweet spot.

"Your turn, Zoe," Natalie said.

"Oh." Zoe hesitated, looking less than self-assured for the first time since she'd arrived. "Well, um . . ."

Idly, Jim wondered if she was carrying a secret, like he and Kelvin were. Could it be that Lord Neon actually sent *three* of his pet projects to the Dare on the same transport?

Just as her silence was growing awkward, a boom filled the sky. Jim peered up as two shining objects dropped through the clouds and plummeted toward the ground.

In a blink, they arrived and halted a foot above the grass, dramatically sending a rush of wind out in every direction. Jim saw them clearly now—two large, smooth silver orbs, one in front of each circle in the grass. Someone in the Spectrum really liked circles.

Looking back and forth between the orbs, Jim chuckled to himself. Zoe glanced sidelong at him.

"What?" she said.

"I only have half a joke so far, but I know it ends with *balls of steel.*"

She might have smirked again. It was too small and happened too quickly to tell. Still hitting the target right between funny and stupid, as expected.

An alert tone emanated from their orb. Pinpoints of light raced across the mirror-polished surface, revealing a complex pattern of seams. When the lights stopped, the orb bloomed open to reveal plush seats with high-g harnesses.

"Well," Jim said. "Our ride, I suppose."

"Nervous?" Zoe asked.

"Oh no, I've always wanted to travel by hamster ball."

The orb didn't scare him. But as soon as he stepped inside, there would be no going back. He would either find Summer's secret file or fail utterly. This wouldn't end until one of those happened. And to do it, he was infiltrating the space fortress of the world's most powerful and revered heroes. In his mind, that needle between Funny and Stupid was tipping in Stupid's direction.

Get. In. The. Hamster ball.

Shaking his head, Jim climbed inside and strapped into a chair. His travel companions followed, their expressions offering varied levels of trepidation and excitement. Even if they weren't hunting for a presumed-dead sister, now they were also locked into this until the end.

When the last harness clicked, the orb refolded and sealed shut, plunging them into a moment of pitch darkness. Then the walls disappeared as if someone had peeled away the outer layer, giving them a full view of the world outside.

"Whoa, this thing is see-through?!" Natalie exclaimed.

"It's a video screen," Jim said. "The power consumption is a dead giveaway."

"Oh," Natalie said, then brightened. "So, you have electrical powers?"

Before Jim could answer, the orb shot skyward as if fired from a railgun. Between heartbeats, the Reaches dropped away until they were two specks beneath his feet.

Jim realized that three people were screaming. One of them may have been him. There was really no way to tell. And with no cameras inside the orb, there definitely wouldn't be any evidence of who did or did not scream like a child. One thing was for sure—if Jim had been screaming, which really there was no definitive proof of, he grabbed hold of himself as the blue sky darkened and became black space.

Kelvin's own scream faded, and he followed it up with a final whoop. "Well, now that was a hoot."

"Best day ever!" Natalie cheered, hands in the air like this was a rollercoaster.

Jim glanced at Zoe. Three people had screamed in a moment of mortal terror, but she may have been the one who kept her dignity. Or maybe not. Who's to say?

She eyed him back, her little smirk resurfacing. "Speaking of balls of steel."

Jim grinned. "I don't have a witty comeback right now, so I'll just say *witty comeback* and let's assume I would have come up with something clever. And . . . whoa."

Suddenly, he was weightless. A look of wonder passed over all four faces as hair and limbs began to float. For the first time in Jim's life, he wasn't on his home planet anymore. Peering back at Earth, he could actually *see Earth*.

"Wow," Zoe breathed.

"Oh, look!" Natalie jabbed her finger in the other direction. "There it is."

The Lighthouse.

For decades it had been a modest facility, roughly the size of an office building. Then, eight years ago, the Spectrum had started building again. Now their base rivaled a skyscraper. An awe-inspiring vision in silver and glimmering white streaked with soft gray, smooth lines and sweeping curves festooned with lights, it looked more like a sculpture than a station.

A central tower formed the spine. It tapered to a staggered point at the bottom and widened toward the top, where it culminated in a clear dome of invisalloy–a transparent metal composite. The edges of each heptagonal invisalloy panel were plated with something like copper, burnished and shining in the sunlight. When seen all at once from a distance, the whole thing resembled a grand cosmic torch.

A ring encircled the tower below the dome, connecting to it via seven massive arms. Like a wheel wrapped around a torch, which didn't really make sense to Jim as an example, but hey, that's what it looked like. He wasn't a space architect.

A . . . sparchitect.

Spacitect?

Focus.

Farther out, seven satellites circled the Lighthouse. What had previously been asteroids were now shaped, partially hollowed, and covered with all manner of technological . . . well, Jim just called them doohickeys, as a gentleman should. Each satellite sat within three concentric rings, all spinning in different directions and at different speeds, and each satellite lit in a different Spectrum color.

"Now, that calls for a wow," Kelvin said, eyes wide and mouth open. "WOW."

As they pulled closer, angling toward a docking bay, an enormous presence grew in Jim's senses. It took him a moment to realize what that feeling was. Rivers of electricity flowed through the Lighthouse–possibly the most massive rush of power in a single place that he'd ever felt. Even greater than the Atherton building.

Do not be impressed. I forbid you to be impressed.

What, at this glorified candle? Please.

You know you can't lie to me, right? I'm literally your brain.

Then literally shut up.

They docked with a soft thunk, and the internal screens went dark. The orb bloomed open to reveal an airlock, into which they exited. When they were all standing in the small sealed room, the orb closed and beams of light washed over them.

"Cool, scanning beams," Kelvin said. "You think they're scanning for threats, or sweeping away bacteria? Or both? Gee, that would be a delight."

Natalie practically swooned. "I feel like Dorothy seeing Oz."

Jim and Zoe exchanged a knowing look. Then Zoe seemed to catch herself and realize who she was having a moment with. She looked the other way.

The beams stopped with a friendly beep.

"Welcome to Mirador, home of the Spectrum, known to all as the Lighthouse," an overwhelmingly pleasant female voice said. "Evildoers beware, and please watch your step as you disembark."

With a heavy *clank-hiss*, the airlock door unsealed. Jim prepared himself to endure some manner of welcome party where he'd have to feign desire to be part of this world. But when the door opened to a large circular chamber, it didn't reveal a party.

It revealed a full-on battle.

Three other orbs had already unloaded. Those heroes were now locked in combat with red-armored, thick-tailed lizard men wielding cannons and blades. Explosions and fireballs and ice sheets and plasma beams flew furiously back and forth across the room among a dozen other powers.

Some unseen force shoved Jim and his group from behind, spilling them into the room and locking the door shut behind them. For a moment, they stood frozen, staring in shock and trying to process the chaos.

A man in purple Roman centurion armor tumbled toward the edge of the battle. Hauling up to his feet, he straightened his plumed green helmet and unsheathed two short swords, their sharp edges glowing with purple energy. As he was about to leap back into the fray, he noticed them.

"Don't just stand there," he shouted. "Help us!"

SEVEN

BATTLE hunger surged through Jim like he hadn't felt for a decade. His first instinct was to dive into the fray.

He put a hand behind him, leaning back until his palm touched the wall. Hopefully, no one would notice him absorbing some of the station's energy to boost his own power. It would be simple to take command of all the electrical conduits running behind these walls and wield them like extensions of his will.

Wait. He froze, remembering his cover. Jim Cranston could only turn things on and off. How would that be any help here? Should he turn out all the lights?

"Turbo-Lizards!" Natalie said. "These are Badland's henchmen. Genetically altered raptors with cybernetic enhancements."

Kelvin pressed against the wall next to Jim. "Badland is a mid-level villain. He almost never leaves New Beijinsk. How would he manage this?"

"Who cares? Let's get to work." Zoe stepped forward, glancing over her shoulder. "You boys coming?"

"We're, um, both Controllers," Kelvin said, indicating himself and Jim.

It was a bit embarrassing, but at least they weren't the only ones. Around the room, a few other heroes stood back–some with hands outstretched, others wearing looks of concentration. Although any parahuman was physically much tougher than a regular person, some power classes were less suited to standing toe to toe and trading punches. They left that to the Strikers and Smashers.

Zoe shrugged. "Well, have fun on the sidelines. Nat?"

Natalie clenched her fists. "Ready!"

The two women leapt forward.

Jim lost track of Zoe almost immediately, but was able to follow Natalie. As he watched, his jaw slowly dropped. Gone were the bright eyes and eager smile. Gone was the star-struck young girl. Natalie shed them like a coat and waded into battle.

As she stepped into the fight, another hero landed a solid kick and knocked an enemy into her path. The Turbo-Lizard righted itself and brought a huge beam cannon to bear on the hero, whose eyes widened in fear.

Cocking back her left arm, Natalie made a fist, which then sprouted a jagged sphere of granite. The rock enveloped her hand like a spiked bowling ball. Shouting, Natalie threw the punch, and with an audible *boom-crunch* she shattered the beam cannon as if it were made of plaster.

The raptor fell back, drew a curved sword, and struck at Natalie's heart. Jim winced when the blade connected, fearing the worst, but sparks flew as it glanced off the rock armor that grew over Natalie's torso.

Her granite fist expanded to become a shield. Her right hand sprouted razor-sharp spikes of obsidian, which she swung to shear off a chunk of her enemy's armor. They danced around each other, trading blows, neither letting up nor giving ground. It was a stalemate until the Turbo-Lizard launched a surprise over-head strike with its powerful tail, driving Natalie to her knees.

Her eyes flashed with fury. The granite shield and obsid-ian blades disappeared. As she regained her feet, Natalie brought both hands together and conjured a cartoonishly huge stone mal-let. Shouting again, she swung. With a *crack*, the Turbo-Lizard flew out of the battle and dropped in a motionless heap.

Jim thought he felt a surge of electricity from Natalie's vanquished foe. But there was so much power flying around the room, it was hard to know for certain.

Another hero toppled onto his back. A Turbo-Lizard stood over the man, wielding two sparking stun batons. That hero was in serious trouble if he didn't move.

Or if someone didn't help him.

Reaching out, Jim grabbed the batons in his mind and switched off their electrical flow. The sparks sputtered and died. In the split second the lizard was distracted by the change, the hero held up his hand. A beam lanced from his palm and struck his enemy square in the chest. The reptile blasted upward and bounced hard off the ceiling, leaving a spiderweb of cracks. When it crashed down, it released an electrical pulse and didn't move again.

Zoe appeared out of the fray and slid up to Kelvin. "Can you make me fully invisible?"

"I can. But it would blind you, since light wouldn't reach your optic nerve."

"Fine, how about these?"

With a casual flourish, Zoe produced a handful of curved, half-serrated throwing knives.

Kelvin shrugged and nodded. "Yeah, no problem."

Jim felt a surge of power from the left. He turned to see a Turbo-Lizard's shock whip catch a tall woman in the back. With a strained cry, she shivered and collapsed. Jim reached out again and shut down the shock whip, buying the hero time to get back up and retaliate.

Kelvin gestured vaguely at the knives, which shimmered and disappeared.

"Thanks," Zoe said, and charged back into the fight.

A Turbo-Lizard fired its jetpack and rose above the battle. Shouldering a massive beam rifle, it took aim at the heroes below. Jim focused on the weapon.

Before he could shut it down, Zoe leapt into the air and sheathed herself in inky blackness. For a heartbeat, her form became a shifting blur. She was in one place, then suddenly in another. The blackness receded with a puff of steam, and Zoe grabbed onto the flying Turbo-Lizard. Planting her knees on its shoulders, she flicked both wrists down toward the main battle. Though there appeared to be nothing in her hands, two Turbo-Lizards jerked as if struck and then dropped.

Blue-white energy arced across their wounds, then went dark. Huh. Weird.

Moving with practiced ease and zero mercy, Zoe plunged an invisible blade into the flying Turbo-Lizard where neck met spine. It went limp and dropped hard, while Zoe became a black blur again and flowed toward another part of the battle.

If Jim's jaw had dropped at Natalie, he absolutely gaped at Zoe. The way she moved . . .

Oh, I'm in trouble, alright.

"Where's the Spectrum?" cried the tall woman that Jim had assisted. "Why aren't they helping?"

"Just focus!" said the purple-armored centurion. "We can do this!"

Actually, the woman had a point. Shouldn't this be a small-time threat for the Spectrum? And this was their sanctuary. So, where were they?

Jim thought back to those surges of power from the collapsing Turbo-Lizards. He made himself slow down and take a second, fresh-eyed look at the battle. Adding everything together, he suddenly had a theory. But focusing his perceptions through the fray was difficult, and he hadn't practiced in so long. How could he figure out if the theory was . . . *hold on.*

"Kelvin, make me invisible."

"You'll be blind."

"I know," Jim said. "That's what I want."

He leaned back once again and covertly pressed his hand against the wall. Shrugging, Kelvin reached out, and everything turned the deepest, darkest black Jim had ever experienced. He swayed for an instant, remnant colors bursting and dancing along his optic nerves, then forced himself to focus.

You're an Electric Controller, he told himself. *Act like it.*

There was no vision to distract him now. Reaching out with parahuman senses, Jim let his mind's eye see all the flows of electricity around him. The conduits behind the walls. The light strips overhead. The points of battery power glowing within weapons and armor. And finally, the signatures that weren't like the others–dozens of them, each pulsing from inside a Turbo-Lizard.

Gotcha.

His theory had been right. Now it was time to end this.

At his base power level, Jim could do this with several enemies at a time. But the fighting was becoming more desperate, so he needed to get them all in one shot.

Concealing his next move would be tricky. No one could discover what he was about to do, or questions would follow. Questions he didn't want to answer. It would put a spotlight on him, and that was the last thing he needed.

Through the connection from placing his hand on the wall, he absorbed a current of the Lighthouse's power. It felt like breathing in life itself, pure energy crackling along his veins. The range, strength, and control of his power grew as he drank it in, as if stretching muscles that he hadn't moved in years.

Now, with every raptor's power signature fixed in his perception, Jim mentally reached out and grabbed them all and gave a command.

Overload.

With a series of loud, static pops, the signatures burst and went dark like blown lightbulbs. Jim heard bulky objects hit the floor. Then, except for heavy breathing, all was quiet.

"Okay, Kelvin," he said.

As he took his hand from the wall, the dark receded. Around the room, the Turbo-Lizards lay in crumpled heaps, smoke wafting from craters in their chests. The pop had been their batteries bursting.

The heroes had taken some damage, but not as much as they should have. Mostly cuts and bruises, nothing broken or even close to life-threatening. Which matched exactly what Jim had figured out.

"What just happened?" Natalie said.

"Pretty sure I know." Kelvin sheepishly raised his hand. When everyone looked in his direction, he nodded toward Jim.

Great. Thanks, buddy. So much for staying under the radar.

Sheathing his blades, the purple centurion stepped closer. "Explain yourself," he demanded in a British accent that was almost too uppity to be real.

"Oh, um, no thanks," Jim said.

Nobody moved or took their eyes off him. Eventually, he acquiesced with a sigh.

"Badland genetically engineers his raptors–they have tech enhancements, but they're mostly organic. But I sensed batteries powering these. If they're machines, that suggests they aren't really enemies and this isn't an attack. It's a test. So I turned them all off. I guess their batteries overloaded when I did that. Also, Kelvin mentioned that Badland operates in New Beijinsk and rarely leaves the city. And it's pretty common knowledge that he considers Geometron his nemesis, so if he were really here, I figured she would be, too."

Some of the hero wannabes looked surprised. Some seemed halfway impressed, others relieved that they hadn't been in real danger. One or two appeared resentful, as if they wished it had been them that "saved" the battle–a sentiment Jim wholeheartedly agreed with.

Natalie was some combination of awestruck and overjoyed. Zoe's gaze was completely inscrutable.

The only reaction that seemed out of place was the purple centurion's. He grimaced as if Jim had personally offended him. Where a few others called out thanks to Jim, the centurion looked as if he wanted to start another fight. Which would only make sense if something else were true.

"Wait." Jim pointed at him. "You're a Prism hero, aren't you? Planted here to watch the test, and maybe to make sure no one actually got hurt."

Now the centurion positively seethed. Instead of throwing a punch like he obviously wanted to, he pressed on his right temple and spoke as a communicator shimmered into view.

Not just any communicator–the special device used by the Spectrum and their Prisms. Jim grinned. He'd been right.

"We're blown. One of *them* figured it out," the purple guy said, dripping with disdain. He cocked his head, listening. "Copy that. Proceed."

There was a heavy clank to Jim's left. He turned as a large section of the wall split to reveal that it had been a blast door all along. There was a wide hallway on the other side, leading deeper into the Lighthouse.

A woman waited there. Tall and lean, with blonde hair peeking out from beneath a helmet and visor, she wore a form-fitting suit of shiny blue and gold. Hanging off her shoulders, the blue cape swayed in the nonexistent breeze.

This was Road Rash, one of the seven Spectrum heroes, and the fastest woman on Earth.

EIGHT

FOR most people with a Traveler power, it was a secondary abil-ity. Something to augment their main power and get them out of danger quickly. Those few with a high-powered Traveler main class tended to make names for themselves. Flyers, Runners, Teleporters, Leapers, Dodgers, Phasers–they were slippery folk, hard to predict or plan for. And the best of them could make even a Smasher think twice.

Road Rash was a blur, moving around the room to wel-come each of them face-to-face as she spoke. For a Runner at her power level, it was just another day at the office. For everyone moving at normal speed, the effect was like being surrounded by a friendly blue-gold tornado while an exuberant voice spoke from every direction at once.

"Hey   everyone   welcome

to outer space and   welcome to   the   Dare

            the vacuum outside will   boil you alive so   don't
open a window hahaha

but we're nice   in here I promise

this is a big day but relax and be

yourself and show   us what you can do   and   everything's
going to be

awesome   as long as you aren't

secretly here for some

nefarious reason

in which case   we'll   of course
discover your secret

and deliver the
smackdown
of justice

anyway my Prism heroes

will give you instructions

and I cannot wait

to see you

all

in

action

BYEEEEEEEEE!"

Then she was gone, leaving the purple guy and two other Prism heroes who'd been flanking her when the door opened. The three of them spread out and began approaching small clusters of heroes to inform them what came next. The other two looked friendly, so of course Jim and his group had to get the purple guy.

"So, yes, the Dare has already begun," he confirmed, shooting a wicked glare at Jim. "I trust no one will sabotage any more of these carefully planned tests."

"You mean *solved*, right?" Natalie asked innocently. "Didn't Jim solve the test?"

The centurion rolled his eyes, ignoring her. Instead, he pulled a handful of small devices from a pouch at his belt and handed one to each of them. They resembled sleek fitness trackers, the band embossed with the symbol of the Spectrum–a stylized, angular torch with a flame on top that morphed between seven colors as Jim studied it from different angles.

"Strap this to your wrist. We call it the Gauge. It will identify you, monitor your activity, and record power flows as you progress through the Dare." He produced a small tablet and tapped on the screen. "I'll check you in now. Do not move until we have finished."

"But what if I have a dance in my heart and I've just *got* to get it out?" Jim asked.

The purple buzzkill sighed, not bothering to look up from the tablet. "I'm syncing your biometric data, which will identify you in my system."

Jim held his breath while the Gauge scanned him. Now they would find out if Lord Neon's scheme could work. Had he really been able to bury the Spectrum's old files on James Riven? Or would this insane quest end before it even began?

The tablet beeped. The centurion pointed at Jim.

"James Cranston, age twenty-eight. Moniker: Interruptor. Class: Electric Controller."

Jim stifled a sigh of relief. The next hurdle was . . . hurdled? Whatever you do to hurdles, he'd done it. Still, it was too fun to keep messing with this guy.

"Actually, no, I'm a human mood ring." Jim placed his fingertip against the centurion's forehead. "I'm sensing you're annoyed right now. And a little gassy."

Purple guy smacked his hand away. "Stop that."

"Well, stop eating all that broccoli, man. Help me help you."

"Hmph. *Minor*. Electric. Controller. Faraday rating 2.1."

"Uh, yep, that's me."

Another smokescreen, courtesy of Lord Neon. That was good. They would underestimate him.

The Faraday Parahuman Power Scale ranged from a barely-there 0.1 to a god-like 10.0. Some called their rating a capacity, a power level, a Faraday rating, or simply a number.

While the terminology was loose, the scale itself was specific. Abilities varied from person to person, but the energy that fueled them did not. Every parahuman made the same energy and "burned" or consumed it to power what they could do. Kind of like calories. The higher a person's energy production, the higher they rated on the scale, and the more powerful their abilities would be.

Jim's actual resting power level was a 3.6, so whatever Lord Neon had done, the ruse included these devices. The Gauge had also missed Jim's . . . other ability, which was doubly good. Very few people knew about that, and it was going to stay that way.

"Interruptor," Kelvin said as if rolling the moniker around in his head. "I dig it."

"You would," the centurion muttered.

Jim aimed his fakest smile at the hero. "And you must be Captain Eggplant."

"Excuse me?"

"Or maybe Admiral Aubergine?"

The centurion puffed out his chest. "*I* am Royal Justice, and *you* have the humor of a peasant."

"Hey, man, there's no shame in guarding the planet's dinner. Someone has to, right? You've got the costume for it."

"These are the colors of my ancient, and famous, family crest. I wonder why you wouldn't recognize them?"

Zoe raised her hand. "Purple armor, green plumed helmet. I'm going to go out on a limb and say it's because you look like King of the Eggplants."

She kept a straight face while Royal Justice fumed. With visible effort, he put a lid on his temper and plowed ahead.

"Kelvin Scott, age twenty-eight. Moniker: Delete. Light Controller, capacity 1.1."

"Hey, super nice to meet you." Kelvin held out his hand. Royal Justice stared at the hand like it was covered in pee until Kelvin lowered it.

"Natalie Yu, age seventeen. Moniker: Marble."

"That's me!" Natalie said, as if she'd won a prize. "Wow. A Prism hero said my name."

"Class: Earth Smasher. Power level . . ." The centurion paused, his eyebrows lifting. "Power level 7.8."

Whoa. That was a big number, and the higher the numbers went, the more rare they became. All eyes turned to Natalie. She blushed and stared at the floor, fingers laced together behind her back.

"It's really not as high as it sounds. And I-I'm still learning how to use it."

"Marble." Zoe nudged her. "I like it."

She brightened. "Thanks. It felt fitting. You know, a tiny thing made of stone."

Royal Justice rolled his eyes. Scanning the screen, he pointed at Zoe. "Zoe Blake, age twenty-six. Capacity 6.2. Class . . ." His eyebrows raised for the second time. "*Multi*-Class. Striker, sub-classes Duelist and Stalker. Traveler, sub-class Dodger. Aethyr augment to . . . to *all* classes and sub-classes.

More raised eyebrows. Wow. These were some seriously tough women.

Out of four Striker sub-classes, Zoe had two, and her Traveler and Aethyr abilities would heighten and complement them. The only Striker sub-classes she lacked were Brawler and Sniper. A suite of powers like hers would mean she had amazing reflexes and agility, superhuman proficiency with weapons and tools (basically anything handheld), and incredible stealth.

She could also augment her powers with Aethyr, that inky black substance, which explained how she moved the way she did. Powers related to that dark energy were incredibly rare, and few truly understood what it really was.

"And your moniker–" The centurion stopped, double- and triple-taking whatever he saw on the tablet. Jaw clenched, he aimed a death glare at Zoe. "Oh, yes. I heard you were coming. How distasteful."

Zoe just stared back at him, as if she knew exactly what he meant and was determined to give no reaction. Interesting.

"Moving on to things that matter, instructions are uploading to your phones," Royal Justice continued. "You are each assigned private quarters to change into your costumes and leave your belongings. Then you'll join the others in the Torch for opening ceremonies. That is all." He turned to leave, but stopped short. "Oh, one more thing. Your Gauge cannot be removed unless unlocked by us. So don't try anything daft. Their tracking is unbeatable."

He said it while burning another glare into Zoe. Then he turned on his heels and stomped toward another group to run through the same routine.

"Wow. What a helpful guy," Kelvin said, apparently unaware that they'd all been insulted.

"Right?" Natalie said. "Everyone here is so nice."

Jim and Zoe exchanged a knowing smile while their new friends gabbed about how great everything in the universe was. Then Zoe caught herself again, and her expression turned stony.

"By the way," Jim said quietly, leaning closer. "This is me, wondering what Captain Eggplant was talking about and exerting heroic self-control in not asking."

"It's nothing I didn't expect," Zoe said, attempting a careless shrug but only half succeeding.

"I just hope the rest of the plant-life doesn't follow his example," Jim said. "No one likes an uppity vegetable."

Zoe eyed him. "You don't like heroes very much, do you?"

"Not particularly."

"Why?"

"Well, for one thing, they actually call themselves heroes. I mean, tacky much? What if I went around telling everyone I'm a godlike pinball player? They'd be annoyed *and* jealous."

Zoe's head tilted. "If you don't want to be one of them, why are you here?"

Jim leaned back, unconsciously moving away from her. That question rode dangerously close to a line he couldn't cross. Not if he wanted to do what he really came here for. He searched for a plausible response but came up empty.

When he didn't answer, Zoe shrugged. "Anyway, let's get into gear and meet up later. I could use some quiet time before it all starts."

The group agreed and parted, each following the directions on their phones. Jim couldn't help glancing covertly at Zoe as she moved away. What was her story, really? Why was she here if Prism heroes didn't want her to be? And what was that lovely scent she was wearing? So many questions, all of them equally important.

No, really, they were.

Shut up.

Jim stood in his quarters, peering awestruck through the invisalloy, into space. Never before had he felt so tiny, so much a part of something bigger than–

He shook himself. "Yikes. That's enough gazing at the wonders of the universe and pondering your own existence."

He moved to the bed, where he'd tossed his bag. Unzipping the top, he set his fake identity's phone on the bedspread and took a moment to scoff once again at the costume Lord Neon had provided. Or, he supposed, it was more of a disguise than a costume, since he wasn't supposed to be himself right now. But if flannel and jeans weren't heroic enough, there was something fundamentally broken in the world.

"Sorry, dude. You can put that on me when I'm dead."

He picked up Lord Neon's phone and let it scan him. Now that he was alone, he could access the instructions the hero had left for him. Hopefully, within the hour, Summer's file would be in his hands. After that, he could find some way to wash out of the Dare and go home.

The phone unlocked. A series of automated commands flashed across the screen, as if the device were peeling away layers of protection, until a box opened and a file popped out. Like a digital strip of paper, it unfurled across the screen.

Follow the green line.

That was it. Jim's instructions for this grand scheme comprised one sentence.

"Seriously? What does that even mean?"

The screen filled with Lord Neon's face.

"Gah!" Jim nearly dropped the phone. "Do you have to make a dramatic entrance every time?"

"You would prefer that we speak in person and risk someone seeing us?"

"Okay, first of all, I don't appreciate you bringing logic into this. Second, what am I supposed to do with *follow the green line*?"

"You're supposed to find the green line, then follow it."

"Let's try this again. Is the green line, like, an electrical wire? A hallway? A sewage pipe? One of those tubes they use at the bank to send me lollipops? At least tell me where to start."

"Begin where and how you choose. It is the searching that will reveal the path."

"Oh, thanks. I was worried you were going to be vague."

"If I revealed more to you now, then you might never find what you seek." Lord Neon looked down, as if examining Jim from head to toe. "You're not wearing the costume."

"Wow, you really are the master of all knowledge. I told you, I'm not trying to be a hero."

"But your alias is."

"You don't understand. If I put that thing on, I'll want to throw myself out an airlock."

"It is not merely a disguise, Jim. I cannot say more." Lord Neon leaned closer. "You trusted me enough to come this far. Trust me a little farther."

The hero's visage faded, replaced by an old photo of Lock and Lode. Jim froze. He knew this picture. His parents had taken it the very first time they wore the costumes, right before going out to be heroes. They were going to take on the world.

"Now, that's a cheap shot."

Closing his eyes, Jim took a moment to breathe, to gather himself, to bury a decade's worth of resentment. Then, before his better judgment could take over, he upended the bag and spilled the costume onto the bed.

"Fine," he muttered. "But I'm gonna be the worst hero ever, just to spite you."

There was no green line. Not that Jim could see yet, anyway. All around him, he could perceive the lines of electrical power sustaining the Lighthouse, but those had always appeared blue-white. So it must be something physical he would have to hunt down.

He stood at the edge of a doorway, but couldn't bring himself to enter the atrium. Most of the wannabes were already gathered there. As soon as he joined them, there would be no going back to a time when they hadn't seen him in this costume.

He wore a zip-up jacket, dark stormy blue with silver threading, as if electricity held it together. It was almost-but-not-quite molded leather, in a style that was almost-but-not-quite biker-like. The black pants tucked into knee-high boots of the same leather-like material and color as the jacket. Jim had to admit it could have been worse, but he missed his flannel.

The Torch's atrium was all kinds of majestic—pretty much the polar opposite of Jim's gritty old world where dilapidated wasn't just a fashion choice, it was a way of life. There were exotic carved stone and fountains and greenery everywhere. Sunlight shone through the polarized invisalloy, glinting off the copper heptagonal edges and making the waterfall sparkle. The whole place smelled fresh, like standing next to a river in a forest untouched by industry.

OmniBots floated to and fro, polishing everything in sight. Jim kept a wary eye on them. Whoever sent those OmniBots to ambush him, could they control these, too?

Seven statues ringed the atrium, each standing a modest five stories tall. Ten stories would have been ostentatious, but five? Well, apparently that was just good taste. The statues depicted members of the Spectrum, each rendered in pale stone with marbling of a color that matched their cape.

Skypuncher of the yellow cape, the powerful yet charming beacon of hope. Supersonic Flyer, Smasher with subclasses Steelskin and Mega-Strength, and who knew what else.

Lord Neon of the violet cape, the shadow of an enigma, who knew things.

Millennia of the green cape, the fearless, uncompromising warrior queen. Stoneskin Smasher, Striker with at least a Brawler sub-class. Leaper traveling power. Bio Controller, specifically self-regeneration, which explained her near-immortal reputation.

Road Rash of the blue cape, who was eccentric in a way that made sense for someone who could run around the world before you even knew she'd moved.

Clarion of the indigo cape, a Sonic Controller who created constructs out of sound waves, sculpting them into anything he desired, and who reportedly had a flare for the dramatic (as a result, some believed, of his alter ego's failed career as a rock star).

Geometron of the orange cape. Half her body was organic, the other half cybernetic. She was the tech nerd of the team, and consistently made *Powered* magazine's annual list of Sexiest Heroes Alive, so she'd gathered quite a following in the cosplay community. It was unclear what kind of parahuman she was, but it didn't seem to matter. Whatever her power, she more than held her own beside the others.

Red Plasma–formerly Plasma until receiving the red cape–was the newest Spectrum hero. The pride of Pakistan, number three all-time Velocity player for the Karachi Heatwave. He was a powerful Blaster, dealing out beams of energy that some guessed were a cross between Radiant and Nuclear. Also a Teleporter, and according to rumor, a competent ballroom dancer.

He replaced Anchor, a much-loved Gravity Controller who had died during the battle with . . . with Framework. Anchor had married Geometron only a year prior to that battle. Some thought she had never seemed quite the same after losing him.

Jim's mind stuttered at the thought, his insides going sour. The same battle had taken Summer, or so they had been told. Yet there was no statue for Lock. Not even a human-sized one.

"Hey, buddy." Kelvin approached, wearing a nondescript gray jumpsuit and a domino mask over his eyes. "Awesome costume."

"Please. I look like a Backstreet Boy."

Kelvin laughed. "Good one! But still, it looks great."

"It totally does!" Natalie appeared, wearing a faded brown hoodie with the blue silhouette of a mountain spray painted across the chest. "The jacket really makes your eyes pop. Hey, why are we all the way back here?"

"I'm waiting for Willy Wonka to show up," Jim said. "If someone's turning into a blueberry, I'd rather it not be me."

Natalie tugged on their arms. "Come on, we've got more friends to make!"

"What about Zoe?" Kelvin said.

"She'll catch up. Let's go!"

Natalie bounced into the atrium with Jim and Kelvin in tow. As soon as they reached the other contestants, she wasted no time hugging and making everyone her best friend. Jim shook a few primary-color-clad hands that wandered his way, but mostly hung back.

I'm not here to make friends, he thought, then mentally kicked himself. That was what every jerk on every reality show said right before they got voted off, proving that they had succeeded in making no friends.

At least try acting like you're here because you want to be.

Fine, but I'm going to complain about it the whole time

I'd expect no less.

"Say, what kind of test do you think they'll give us?" Kelvin said. "Will it be, like, puzzles and stuff, or are we supposed to just get in the arena and . . ." He glanced at Jim and trailed off.

"And what?" Jim asked.

Kelvin didn't answer. In fact, one by one, everyone stared at Jim and went silent–some with shock, others with thinly veiled outrage. A few even drew weapons.

"Aw, man," Jim said. "My costume really does suck, doesn't it? I knew it."

"Whoa," Kelvin breathed. "So, that's her secret."

Jim realized then that no one was actually looking at him. They were looking directly past him. He turned.

Zoe had arrived. Only, she wasn't Zoe anymore.

Three-piece suit in dark gray with pinstripes. Black trench coat and fedora. Tall black boots. She could have stepped out of a noir detective novel if it weren't for the red-lensed goggles, the fancy black mask covering the bottom half of her face, and the high-tech gloves with subtle red lights tracing the fingertips.

Kelvin had been right. Whoa, indeed.

It turned out Zoe Blake was famous as her alter ego, Moxie. And Moxie wasn't a hero.

She was a villain.

NINE

"VILLAIN!" someone spat.

Zoe stopped half a dozen paces from the crowd and waited, as if she'd known this moment was coming. She appeared completely at ease. Then again, most of her face was covered, so really it was anyone's guess. But her posture was strong, as if she wore her reputation like armor.

Despite being out of the hero game for a decade, Jim actually knew about Moxie. She had gone active right around the time he quit. In an impressively short amount of time, she had established herself as one of the world's best thieves for hire.

As far as he knew, she'd never been the kind of villain who wanted to destroy cities or hurt people. She was just good at her job, which happened to be morally gray. And apparently no one had ever caught her—which, now that Jim thought about it, might be one reason so many heroes hated her. Because she was better.

Is it weird that Villain Zoe is even hotter than Decaf Zoe?

No, that's just good taste.

Oh, good.

"You're not welcome here!" A man built like a cargo van stepped forward, his scowl contrasting with the bright yellow leotard. "I don't know how you got here, but you have one chance to leave before things get–"

Flashes of light in seven colors burst from all directions. Trumpets and clashing cymbals rang out joyously, bright tones reverberating off the walls, while an invisible choir belted out an angelic melody, until every cacophonous note merged and distilled into a shredding electric guitar solo.

Then the Spectrum was there, all seven of the world's greatest heroes standing in the middle of the Torch, on a raised platform that had not been there an instant before. Seven Prism heroes stood behind them.

Front and center, Clarion cast his arms out wide. While the light and sound faded, he pumped a fist in the air and gave a long, power-amplified shout.

"HUZZZZZAAAAAAAAH!"

His voice crested, practically rattling the invisalloy panels overhead. He pulled the fist slowly down to his chest like this was the climax of a dramatic one-man show.

"BEHOLD!" he declared. "YOUR HEROES HAVE–"

"Nope. That's it." Geometron placed a firm hand on Clarion's shoulder and guided him back from center stage. "You're done now. Thank you for that . . . dramatic introduction, master of all sound."

Clarion looked dismayed, but seemed to get the message and took his place farther back. He stood next to Lord Neon, who never looked in Jim or Kelvin's direction, as if they were just two faces in the crowd.

Nice control, LN. It's almost like you've done this before.

Millennia took center stage and peered at the waiting crowd. She stood as straight and taut as razor wire, her eyes weighing and measuring them like a warrior evaluating a rack of weapons.

"Moxie is here at our invitation," she said without preamble, in a tone that brooked no debate. "You will treat her like any other Dare contestant. Who are you–who are any of us–to discourage a thief from choosing a better path? Accept it and move on."

"Retrieval specialist," Zoe said under her breath.

Jim flinched. She was standing next to him now. He hadn't even noticed her moving.

"What's the difference?" he asked.

Zoe pressed a button on a tiny device behind her left ear. The mask-and-goggles combo peeled away from her face, folding in on itself until it packed away inside the device.

"Thieves take anything from anyone," she replied. "Professionals get paid, and they have standards."

On the platform, Millennia continued. "Some heroes last a lifetime, some only a year. They retire, or die, or discover that a life this hard is not for them. So, as guardians of this world, we must be constantly looking to the future, watching for those who have what it takes to offer something more. Because we never know when the best of us may fall. So, thank you for being here, for taking on this challenge. One day, you may help save the world. But first, you . . . you must . . ."

Her speech ground to an awkward halt. She clenched her jaw, as if she were trying to stop herself from saying the next words. Oddly, when Jim looked past her at the other heroes on the platform, they struggled as well. They clenched fists, squared their shoulders like they were waiting to be punched, and a few expended physical effort to keep their lips together.

". . . you must demonstrate that you're prepared to handle the challenges this life will throw at you every day," Millennia said all at once, her words rushing out as if they'd been held by a dam and then burst free. She rattled her head as if to clear stars.

Jim exchanged a puzzled look with Kelvin. He had noticed it, too.

"What is the Dare?" Millennia waved and a huge wireframe hologram of the Lighthouse appeared in the air. A marker blinked at the top, where they stood in the atrium. "The group that you traveled here with is now your team. You'll begin here, in the Torch, and your challenge is to make it *here*."

Another marker appeared on the hologram, this time at the very bottom of the Lighthouse. The last level at the narrow, staggered-point tip.

"The first seven who make it will be invited into a Prism. If your team makes it first and you are fewer than seven, you will all be chosen. If you're on the next team to arrive, you will determine among yourselves who takes the remaining slots. Either way, the first seven to scan your Gauge with the reader on the final door will join us."

Millennia nodded to Geometron, who took over.

"As we speak, maps and other data are uploading to your phones," she said. "Used wisely, they will guide you to your goal. Part of the Dare is testing how you leverage this information to win."

Even with his low expectations, Jim had to admit this seemed like kind of an easy challenge. Get from this place to that place, and be faster than your opponents. Although he wasn't really here for the Dare, he couldn't help feeling disappointed. These were supposed to be the world's greatest heroes. Shouldn't the Dare be something spectacular?

"Wait, that's it?" said the human cargo van in the yellow leotard. "Sounds easy enough. We'll get it done!"

He pumped his fist in the air. His team cheered around him, exchanging high fives like they were a high school football team going for the state championship. Jim felt torn—should he smirk about the jock in spandex, or feel disappointed in himself because he actually agreed?

"You'll find that . . . the . . . the Dare is . . . m-m-much . . ." Geometron was doing it this time, only worse. She shook visibly, as if it were taking all her strength to keep from finishing that sentence.

The same effect passed through every hero on stage. Clarion touched his comm and fell to his knees, as if overexerted. Jim exchanged an uneasy look with his team. Murmurs passed between the other contestants. If anyone had missed it before, now they saw that something wasn't right.

Static filled Jim's head, sharp as a piercing wail. Then it was gone in a flash, leaving another sensation in its wake. Suddenly, he knew.

"Their headsets," he gasped, though too quietly for anyone to hear.

The comms worn by every Spectrum and Prism hero. A giant surge of power had forced its way through them. Now the heroes stopped struggling, and their faces all wore the exact same glower.

Red Plasma stepped forward. He stared down at the contestant in yellow as if one of them was a hawk and the other a fish. Jim's insides clenched. Something was *very* wrong.

"There is one other element to the Dare. The most important one." Red Plasma raised his open palms and conjured two glowing red orbs of energy. "Today, you go home a Prism hero . . . or you don't go home at all."

The orbs became beams. Lancing out, they intersected on the yellow leotard, and he burst into individual atoms. Vaporized.

Shocked cries rang out. Contestants fell back from the platform in horror.

Jim felt frozen in place. He shot a panicked look at Lord Neon, but the hero stood on stage like a statue, offering no reaction. Had he known this was going to happen?

Skypuncher stepped forward, his powerful voice carrying over the noise of the panicking crowd. "Be smart, be fast, and be ruthless," he said, every drop of charm replaced by malevolence. "Welcome to the Dare, and may God have mercy on your souls."

At that instant, everyone flinched as their Gauge tightened enough to hurt. The release latch fused, locking the device onto their wrists.

"Prepare to be hunted." Millennia pointed at the terrified crowd. "GO!"

The atrium turned from panic to pandemonium.

TEN

SHOUTING and blasts of heat and flashes of light and a myriad of crazy explosive powers rocked the atrium. Jim sprinted for an exit with his team, concentrating ahead and pointedly not looking over his shoulder. If they could find a quick path down through the Lighthouse, they might have a chance of surviving.

They were getting close to the open doorway when everything went wrong. A loud klaxon blared. The enormous door began to slide shut with a heavy mechanical rumble.

Something behind them popped and crackled. A silvery white beam of cold shot past Jim, barely missing his head. The air around the beam crystallized as if someone had weaponized a snowstorm.

"Ice Blaster," Zoe called, glancing over her shoulder. "It's Solstice!"

Jim couldn't resist seeing for himself. He turned to see a woman flying toward them, covered in ice and sparkling like a glass figurine. Her chest insignia glowed brighter as she powered up for another attack.

The team dodged and juked as they ran, trying to make themselves more difficult targets. A barrage of cold beams followed in quick succession, painting the floor and the walls around them.

"I'll get the door!" Natalie called.

Jim had no choice but to believe her. Everything was happening too fast to question or doubt. If Natalie was handling the door, the rest of them would have to deal with their hunter. He whipped around, having no clue how he was going to fight a Prism hero *and* maintain his cover.

He didn't have to worry about it, because a cold beam struck him like a sledgehammer and knocked him off his feet.

Get up get up get up keep moving

I know geez shut up

Fortunately, the jacket seemed to have absorbed most of the attack. Aside from impacting the floor, he actually felt fine. The bitter cold was still trying to seep into his bones, but apparently that also had an upside, because he was feeling more alert and aware of his own power.

Which was how he sensed a weakness in Solstice. The symbol on her chest plate wasn't glowing because of her power–something inside it ran on batteries. Jim's best guess was that Solstice needed a regulator to help focus and control her ability. He'd seen something like it with other Blasters. Focusing all that chaotic energy was not easy.

Rolling up to his knees, Jim stretched his hand toward Solstice and commanded the batteries to shut down. She gasped and her symbol went dark.

Kelvin struck next, turning her head invisible, which also blinded her. She yelped in surprise and her flight path dipped toward the floor.

Zoe turned black with Aethyr and leapt high. As Solstice flew beneath her, she twisted into a downward spin-kick and knocked the hero out of the air. Solstice dropped and Zoe followed her down, kicking again and bouncing her off the floor. Solstice slid to a halt, sprawling half-dazed on the floor, while Zoe landed in a crouch and the blackness receded with a puff of steam.

"Wow," Jim said, standing. "Uh, go team?"

Zoe stalked past him. "Celebrate later."

She had a point. Jim spun toward the door in time to see Natalie go to work. The giant steel thing was almost closed and showed no signs of stopping.

Diving forward, Natalie tucked into a ball. With a sound like a landslide, she encased herself in a huge spherical boulder. Somehow, she picked up speed and slammed into the door with an earsplitting *clang*. The metal caved in and halted, unable to slide shut.

"Move!" Zoe said.

Jim and Kelvin followed Zoe and Natalie through the last sliver of open doorway. Jim dove through last, just in time for another cold beam to strike the wall beside his head.

Solstice yelled something unintelligible and stumbled to her feet, regulator sparking fitfully. Jim could feel her communicator surging like before, stoking her rage. Raising both hands, she powered up for a monster blast. If it landed, she could freeze the door enough to shatter it. Then things would get much worse.

Above the door, there was a conduit glowing brightly. Acting purely on instinct, Jim crooked his index finger at the spot. The conduit ripped through the wall, flailing like a whip, and the sparking end smacked into the hero's flank. Solstice fell to her knees with a heavy grunt.

Zoe's hand flicked out. A dart struck Solstice in the chest, then burst into a net that wrapped tightly around her, trapping her arms against her torso. A second dart latched onto her neck and gave a single red pulse of light. She stiffened and toppled once again.

Natalie approached the caved-in door and kicked with a leg sheathed by stone. Her kick bent it back the opposite way, fixing the giant dent enough for the door to move. Squealing and scraping, the steel cried in protest but finally closed.

"Yeah!" Jim cheered, pointing at Solstice through the closed door. "Now is the winter of *your* discontent!"

No one laughed, which made sense, as they had almost died. Still, it felt good to gloat a little.

"In retrospect," Zoe said. "Jim, you should probably have handled the door, and Natalie should have fought Solstice."

Jim nodded. Now that his blood was simmering down, he saw she was right. With a simple command, he could have stopped the door from closing, and Natalie's rock armor could have stood up to the ice blasts. He glanced sidelong at Zoe, who barely seemed out of breath or even that bothered by what had just happened. Maybe being a thief–er, retrieval specialist–meant she got chased and shot at a lot.

"Good point," Kelvin said. "We haven't exactly gotten to practice being a team."

"Whew!" Natalie leaned back against the door and wiped her brow. "That was a nice move with the wire, Jim. It bought me time. I didn't know you could do that."

Aw, crap. Jim Cranston shouldn't *be able to do that.*

"As much as I'd like to take credit, I think your human-boulder trick knocked it loose. Or we have the gods of not being vaporized by heroes on our side." He pointed to a nearby stairwell–a good distraction from talking about his powers. "Let's get off this level."

Leading the way, he hurried down one level. He almost kept going down another flight, wanting to get as far away from the battle as possible, but stopped short.

There was a door on this level. A green door.

Follow the green line.

Could this be a place to start?

"I don't know about you guys, but I need to get my bearings." Jim gestured at the door. "Feel like hiding in terror for a few minutes?"

Zoe nodded. "We need to plan our next move."

Natalie and Kelvin agreed, so Jim opened the door and followed them in, making sure to lock it behind them. They found themselves in a small server room with a handful of blinking racks and a pair of control terminals. The opposite wall had another door with a sign reading *Utility Closet.*

"Okay, first things first." Jim pointed at each of their wrists. "Off, off, off, off." Their Gauges deactivated. "Now they can't track us. I hope."

"Handy power," Zoe muttered.

"You should see me in a dance club," Jim said. "Fun fact: *any* light can be a strobe light if you try hard and believe in yourself."

"I can't believe this," Natalie said, sounding heartbroken, as if her childhood dog had bitten her. "I just can't believe it."

"I know," Jim said. "*And* there was no gift basket in my room. What kind of a dump is this?"

The others gave him flat looks.

He held up his hands. "I make jokes when people try to murder me."

"It's okay, buddy," Kelvin said. "I think we all just . . ."

He kept talking, falling into quiet conversation with the others, but Jim didn't hear it. He scanned the room, his mind on his own private quest. If there had been significance to the green door, he wasn't spotting any clues. Unless the green line was digital?

He approached a terminal. On a hunch, he fished Lord Neon's phone out of his pocket and waved it near the fingerprint scanner. The scanner flashed green and the screen came to life, already logged into what looked like an admin account.

That guy really thought of everything. Too bad he didn't also warn me about . . . what was it, again? Oh, right, all the murdering.

He tapped the keys, digging for anything related to Summer Riven. The search revealed a file with her name, but it was only basic personal information and a general service record. At the bottom, though, the file cut off mid-sentence with a huge digital stamp that said REDACTED in red. Of course. Couldn't make this too easy, now could they?

He searched for anything about a green line, but most of the results were mundane and meaningless. The only halfway interesting results pertained to Millennia, since she wore the green cape. None of it was relevant, though, unless she was hiding the green line somewhere under that armor. Which seemed unlikely.

Then he found something. Not what he was searching for, but given the recent turn of events, a significant discovery. The master control program for the station's escape pods. According to the diagram, there was a single-person pod a dozen yards from this room.

A hero wouldn't even consider it. But Jim Riven was no hero. He could excuse himself for some made-up reason, stroll to the pod, and launch himself back to Earth. No one would blame him if they were being honest with themselves. He didn't sign up to be hunted for sport. He didn't even sign up for the Dare, technically.

Survival instincts could be an ugly beast. Jim sat at the terminal, vacillating between the intense longing to live and the innate need to *not* be a punk and slink away.

If he took that pod, he would live. But he would also never know the truth about Summer. There was no way he could make it back here again, not after this. She would be forever beyond his reach. The very thought felt like having her die all over again.

Then there was . . . *them*. Jim glanced at the band of misfits he'd somehow fallen in with. They talked quietly among themselves, strategizing but also subtly trying to comfort each other, affirming that they would all make it. These were genuinely good people.

They had actually wanted to be here. And before this was over, they just might need Jim if they were going to survive.

"Hey, what has two thumbs and knows we can do this?" Kelvin pointed both thumbs at his own chest. "This guy."

Jim grinned to himself. *Well, that settles it. There's no way I can abandon such a natural comedic genius.*

Like it or not, it seemed he was fully in the game now. He would hunt for the green line, searching secretly for the truth about Summer. But more than that, he would keep his team alive until the end. Until they beat the Dare or died trying.

Aw, look at you, making good choices like a–

Don't you say it, brain, don't you dare.

–like a hero.

Call me that again and I'll stab you with a shrimp fork.

"How could this happen?" Zoe said, quietly desperate. "I'm trying to go straight, and now I learn the Spectrum is secretly evil?"

"That isn't what's happening." Jim left the computer and rejoined his team. "You know how they were acting so weird at first?"

Zoe nodded. "Almost like they couldn't speak."

"Or were trying not to," Natalie said.

"Yeah. Well, I felt something when that was happening. Their comms were getting these huge bursts of power, like something was supercharging them."

"What could that do?" Kelvin snapped his fingers. "Wait. Don't those comms also have a telepathic element?"

Jim nodded. "They do. And if someone figured out how to turn it against them, who knows what they could do?"

"If that's true," Zoe said with dread. "Someone out there is strong enough, and smart enough, to take control of the entire Spectrum."

There was a moment of silence as that sunk in. Even if they were able to survive the Spectrum, what if the power behind all this came out to play? Would their little ragtag bunch stand a chance?

Thump.

If they hadn't fallen quiet, they might never have heard the sound. Now, though, four heads whipped toward the utility closet.

They traded nervous looks. Something was in here with them.

"It could be an OmniBot," Natalie whispered.

Jim shook his head. "There's no electrical flow."

"We'll check it out together," Zoe said.

"Please don't hold it against me if I scream," Kelvin said.

Clustered together, they approached the door, momentarily forgetting that they were all parahumans. When they reached the closet, they all hesitated.

Zoe expelled a quick breath, grabbed the handle, and whipped the door open. Everyone fell a step back, fists up, ready to strike or scream or probably both.

"Wait!" A stocky, bearded black man recoiled, throwing his arms up. "Wait, don't kill me! I . . ." Catching sight of Jim, he stopped short and his arms dropped. "Bartender?"

Jim gaped. Only now, as his heartbeat returned to normal, did he recognize the man in the jumpsuit.

"Eli?!"

ELEVEN

"**YOU** said you were a custodian at Atherton," Jim said.

"Actually, I said I was *the* Custodian, capital-C. And this name-tag?" Eli thumped the square embroidered on his chest. "It projects something different for everyone. Essentially, you saw what you wanted to."

"Why did he call you Bartender?" Natalie asked.

"He's been coming to Versus, my bar in Highreach. It's where we met."

Zoe studied him. "So, you're the new owner."

"You've been there?"

"Once, a few years back. I don't remember seeing you."

"Not being noticed is kind of my thing." Jim grinned at her costume. With the goggles and mask peeled back, she looked like someone out of a Raymond Chandler novel. "Did you go there with Philip Marlowe after cracking a big case?"

Zoe shook her head, pursing insanely full lips, but she couldn't hide a smile. "You really are an idiot."

"Hey, I get it. Prohibition was tough on all of us. I only survived because I found this weird falcon. It was from Maltese, or made of Maltese, or tasted like Maltese, I don't know, but everyone seemed to want it."

"I've heard of you," Natalie said to Eli. "Most people think the Lighthouse caretaker is a myth. You're kind of the caretaker for the Spectrum, too, right?"

"I keep this place running. Sometimes I keep the heroes running, too. They have high-stress jobs and it helps to talk to someone."

"So, you must know this place pretty well," Kelvin said.

Eli nodded. "Been here since the beginning, so yes. Also, I'm an Enviro Sensor, which helps me do my job."

"A what sensor?" Jim asked.

"I absorb data about my environment," Eli explained. "I sort of sense information. It helps me find and fix issues–which, on a station like this, come up often."

"Ah," Jim said. "So, should we call you the Custodian, or . . . ?"

"Eli is fine. We're all friends here, I hope."

"That depends," Zoe said. "Did you know this hunt was going to happen?"

"Or what's really going on?" Kelvin added.

"There, you have me at a loss. I've sensed for a while that something wasn't right, but I could never figure out where it was leading. The only thing I've determined for sure is that the source of the corruption is their comms."

"We sort of figured that," Natalie said. "Or Jim did, anyway."

"But that doesn't tell us their endgame," Zoe said. "Or how to stop it."

"There is another option," Eli offered. "If you can finish the Dare and survive until the end, you might find answers. Maybe even confront the puppet master behind all this." He stood straighter. "I'll make a deal with you. Bring me along, protect me from the hunters, and I'll lend you my knowledge. Perhaps together we'll have a chance of beating the Dare and saving everyone, including the Spectrum."

A man with intimate knowledge of the Lighthouse? They couldn't agree fast enough. No one would suspect they'd have this kind of resource, and the faster they finished the Dare, the more people they could save.

Privately, Jim agreed for a second reason. Someone with Eli's knowledge and ability might be able to help him find the green line, wherever and whatever it was. He'd just have to be subtle about asking.

Everyone's phone buzzed. Whipping them out of various pockets, they stared at Skypuncher's face on their screens.

"Apparently, a few have decided you no longer wish to compete in the Dare, and are attempting to use the escape pods. That's disappointing and not how the game works. We have a strict "no cowards allowed" policy on the Lighthouse. So, you want out? You got it."

His face disappeared, replaced by a red number five.

Five became four.

Four became three.

"Oh, no," Zoe breathed.

Two.

One.

Their screens went dark and there was a series of distant booms. The Lighthouse shuddered.

"Dear God," Eli said. "They must have locked those people in the pods and activated the self-destruct."

Jim suppressed a shiver. If he had followed his baser instincts, he would have been among them.

"People really are dying." Natalie sniffled, wiping away a tear. "They're not going to stop, are they? Not until we're all dead."

All Jim wanted was to run into Eli's closet, slam the door shut, and wait for this to be over. For someone else to charge into mortal danger and save everyone.

But for all he knew, that someone was *them*. This was no Warded Zone–people were getting hurt for real. And, crazy enough, Jim's secret past as a teenage hero might mean he had more experience than the average Dare contestant. Closing his eyes, he worked to gather every shred of tattered, under-used courage.

"Then the faster we move, the more we can save," he said. "I hope."

Zoe nodded. "We make a plan, then we go to work."

Unlocking his phone, Jim called up the Lighthouse map. "So, Eli. Where would you go next?"

TWELVE

THE green door swung open. Jim and his makeshift team–larger by one now–aimed for the stairwell, moving as quickly and quietly as possible. Somewhere in the distance, there was shouting and the sound of metal on metal. Wannabe heroes were clashing with corrupted heroes, and the results weren't going to be pretty.

They crept down one flight, where Eli peered in all directions before leading them across another hallway. Heads on a swivel, watching and listening for any possible threat, the team paced behind him until he stopped at . . . a solid wall.

"Oh, good. You found a wall," Jim said. "We're saved."

Eli touched the wall on a spot that seemed like any other. A pinpoint of light appeared and traced a rectangle in the surface, which popped open to reveal a utility panel.

Kelvin gave Jim a nudge. "Hey, when is a door not a door? When it's–"

"I will stab you if you finish that sentence," Zoe said.

"Oh, sorry, I'm making too much noise."

"No, but puns are the lowest form of humor. You're better than that."

"Discount Sam Spade is right," Jim said. "Why make puns when we could make limericks about how we're all going to die horribly?"

Eli shook his head–probably wondering whether he'd struck the right bargain after all–and flipped a switch. Another pinpoint of light appeared and traced another rectangle in the wall, this one bigger. When the four sides completed, the rectangle opened to reveal a tunnel big enough for two people to crawl through side by side.

"I doubt any other teams know about the Shran tubes, so the Spectrum has no reason to search them," Eli said. "We'll take these down one level, make a quick stop, then resume our quest for the best way to get to the lower levels safely."

Eli ducked into the tunnel and crawled forward. Natalie and Kelvin eyed each other, shrugged, and followed him side by side. Which left Jim and Zoe to bring up the end. They slipped in behind their teammates, and Jim closed the hatch.

As they crawled, he mentally reviewed what Eli had shared before they left their hiding place. Remembering those bits of knowledge might make the difference between surviving and . . . well, not surviving.

"Right now, we're one level beneath the Torch," Eli had said, pointing at the phone screen as he narrated. "This level is for guest quarters and events, anything public-facing for when non-heroes visit. One level below us, we have the docking bays where you arrived. Two down from here–that's the largest level, the one with the ring around it. Hero quarters are in the ring and the Spectrum command center–what we call the Spark–is in the central spire."

"Command center," Zoe had said. "Sounds like where we need to go."

"On the contrary." Eli had pointed to the docking bay level. "There's an important room here that you didn't get to see. That's our first goal."

"Why go only one level down?" Natalie said. "Shouldn't we try to move faster?"

"I need to pick something up. Something that may prove useful."

"*Gotta agree with my friends here,*" Kelvin had said. "*Wouldn't a command center be better than a docking bay?*"

"*Trust me,*" Eli had said. "*I'll explain more on the way.*"

He hadn't explained more yet, but there wasn't much to do about it now. They were already stuffed into a secret passage.

"I wonder if we'll run into Oompa Loompas," Jim muttered.

He thought he'd said it only to himself, but Zoe must have heard.

"If we find a chocolate river, it's mine," she said.

Jim glanced over at her, but she kept her eyes forward. He was halfway to having a response when distant sounds echoed down the Shran tube. Explosions, ripping metal, what may have been screams, and then silence. When the echoes faded, they took with them all the words he'd been planning to say.

"Um," he said, and paused to clear his throat.

Come on, get it together. If you act afraid, you'll be afraid.

Just say something, anything, to change the subject from imminent peril.

"So, what kind of things did you like to steal?" he asked, then winced.

Natalie made an offended sound. Kelvin glanced back at him with a wow-did-you-really-say-that expression.

Now Zoe looked at him. While she didn't seem angry, she also didn't respond.

"I'm not judging," Jim added. "I don't have an axe to grind like Captain Eggplant did. It's just that I don't have any personal experience with the thieving world. I've never even been burgled. Which is too bad, because it's fun saying burgled. *Burgled.*"

"Jim," Eli called.

"Burgled?" Jim replied.

"We're here."

"Got it, shutting up now." In a whisper, he added, "Burgled."

Eli pressed his hand against the hatch at the end of the tube. "I don't sense anyone nearby."

He pressed a button next to the door. It popped open with a soft thunk. The team crawled out after Eli, Jim once again closing the door behind them. Still offering no real explanation, Eli started forward without looking over his shoulder. Apparently, he expected them to stay close.

They followed him around a large ring-shaped corridor, stepping through segments separated by open blast doors. Jim sensed heavy power flowing to them, ready to slam shut on command. As they circled the ring, they passed immense windows looking out onto the diamond-studded black of space, two of the support satellites, and a bright sliver of Earth.

They neared an entrance to one of the docking bays. Jim expected Eli to turn that way, but he kept going and passed it by.

The central column–what Jim thought of as the donut hole in this ring-shaped corridor–held four lifts, each facing a docking bay across the hall. The space inside the donut hole was huge, though, and until now Jim hadn't considered what else it might contain aside from elevators.

He told himself to stop thinking of this corridor as a donut. He was hungry enough already.

Eli stopped at large double doors set into the donut hole. Er, the central column. He placed his hand on a palm reader, which flashed and beeped an affirmation, and the doors slid open with a pleasant hiss.

"This is normally part of the welcome tour," he said as they stepped inside. The doors shut behind them. "But the Spectrum was eager to begin the Dare as soon as possible. Which, in retrospect, sounds a bit ominous."

Natalie gaped, trying to stare everywhere at once. "What is this place?"

Jim hoped his expression was more nonchalant, but he doubted it. Not even a practiced sense of ironic detachment could have prepared him for this.

"We call it the Reliquary," Eli explained. "Artifacts from some of the Spectrum's foremost exploits in protecting the world."

"You mean trophies," Zoe said.

Eli acquiesced. "I like to think of them as reminders. But you could call some of them trophies."

Zoe wasn't wrong, but *trophies* didn't fully capture what Jim was seeing. He might have said *wonders*. Though, if he said something so naïve out loud, he'd have no choice but to let the Spectrum toss him into space.

In row after row, there were dozens–no, hundreds–of invis-alloy cases of varying size, all lit by spotlights from above.

An ancient staff inlaid with ivory and sapphires. Two suits of armor–one slim and sleek, the other massive and imposing–each powered by a glowing yellow jewel set in the helmet. A revolver straight out of the American Old West, unremarkable except that the space around it seemed to warp. A pair of round spectacles with silver wire frames and obsidian black lenses. Jim saw these and more in only the first few seconds.

Eli must have loved this place, too. As he led them deeper into the Reliquary, he couldn't seem to resist pointing out favorite pieces.

A huge sledgehammer, bulky steel festooned with rivets, with a hole in the top. "The Overkiller's weapon of choice–a war hammer with a built-in rocket launcher."

A silver pocket watch with delicate scrollwork on the casing, its insides spread around it in individual pieces. "This just showed up here one day. No one knows how."

A slim dual-edged sword. Instead of the typical steel, this one had ripples of shimmering black along the length of the blade. It almost looked alive. "Dark Sympathy, a jian sword once wielded by the Chaos Merchant. This is the closest we've ever come to capturing the man himself. The blade is inlaid with Aethyr, which we still don't know how he accomplished, or what he used it for."

A peanut butter and jelly sandwich, glowing orange, with a single bite missing. "Don't ask, and *don't* eat it."

At several points, there were breaks in a row of cases, making way for larger artifacts. Like a chunk of concrete rubble, which Jim thought he recognized as part of a bridge. Skypuncher had single-handedly kept it from collapsing until everyone was safe on solid ground.

Kelvin pointed to a six-wheeled vehicle, like a cross between a very old school bus and a very old tank. "Now, that looks like fun."

"Ah, the Kettle, transport of the original Spectrum," Eli said. "Armor, wheels, and an engine. In the old days, they used to ride it into battle. We still keep it hooked to a battery so we can start the engine and let people hear it rumble."

"This place is amazing," Natalie whispered reverently. "Good thing the bad guys don't know this is all here."

"Not to worry," Eli said. "This stuff is useful, but no threat on a grand scale. They keep all the truly world-ending stuff where no one will ever see it, or even learn it exists." Toward the center of the Reliquary, he stopped in front of a case. "Ah, here we are."

Eyebrows raised all around. Was this really what they made the big detour for?

"It's . . . a whistle," Zoe said.

"Looks like the one my old gym teacher had," Kelvin added.

"Cool, magical gym teacher powers," Jim said. "If we run into Skypuncher, we can order him to run laps."

"How will this help us win?" Natalie said.

"It's called the Echo Chamber, and I said it *may* prove useful." Eli looked at Natalie and gestured to the case. "Marble, would you do the honors?"

Natalie gave a determined nod and cocked back her fist. "Right. Step back, everyone."

There was a rumbling sound like rolling rocks. Natalie's fist became a globe-sized gray boulder. She swung and the case shattered.

She gave a satisfied sigh. "I really love doing that."

"I believe you," Eli said. Snatching up the Echo Chamber, he looped the tether around his neck and tucked the whistle into his jumpsuit. "Let's go."

"Wait," Kelvin said. "We're surrounded by a lot of useful stuff. Shouldn't we, I don't know, take a few things with us? We're trying to survive, after all."

Eli eyed him like a schoolteacher preparing to scold a child who asked why they can't eat the gum they found on the bottom of the desk. "You're proposing everyone just grab items that are dangerous enough to be stored here–items that you've never seen and have not trained for–and use them in an enclosed container floating in the vacuum of space?"

Kelvin grimaced and studied the floor, thoroughly chastised.

Jim raised his hand. "If the answer is yes, I call the peanut butter sandwich."

"Let's move on," Eli said as if he hadn't spoken, and led them toward the exit.

Once again, Jim brought up the rear of the team, keeping an eye behind them in case anything lurked in the shadows. He cast his power sense to and fro, scanning for unusual fluctuations. A little advance warning might just keep them alive.

He noticed two things.

First, a stretch of wall to his left stood out because of how much it *didn't* stand out. Power raced behind pretty much every wall in the Lighthouse . . . except for this spot, which was a dead zone. And not only the wall, but a rectangular space behind it as well. Jim thought back to Eli's statement–the public would never see the most dangerous items. Maybe they kept them in that blank space.

Second, a display case stood out because when they'd entered the Reliquary, it had contained an artifact. And now, as they were leaving, the case was empty.

THIRTEEN

THE Reliquary doors slid closed behind them. As they clicked shut, Jim stopped in his tracks.

"Wait," he said, pointing to a section of the corridor wall. "Power flow just rerouted . . . right there."

"I sense no heroes," Eli said.

"It's not heroes. It's . . ." Jim trailed off, but knew in his gut that he'd felt this type of power flow before. Then the memory clicked. "We need to go now."

Twelve pinpoints of light traced along the wall to create twelve large rectangles. In unison, they popped open to eject their contents.

"Oh, hey, it's the OmniBots," Kelvin said. "These things are cute."

"*Not* cute," Jim insisted. "Wait, don't–"

Kelvin patted the nearest machine's head like it was a pet. "Hey there, little guy."

It jabbed a stun gun into Kelvin's flank. Screaming, he collapsed and shuddered like he was being electrocuted. Which he was.

In the time it took for him to fall, the other OmniBots deployed weapons and swarmed. Mayhem exploded across the corridor.

Lunging for the nearest machine, Jim slipped past the gout of flames it tried to fry him with, slapped his hands on the casing and circled around behind it. *Sssssshhhhhh quiet* he said in his mind, pushing the command through the machinery on waves of his power. The OmniBot obeyed, retracting the flamethrower and awaiting instructions.

The next closest OmniBot spun in his direction. Tagging Jim with a targeting laser, it deployed a plasma cutter and fired a beam straight at his head.

"Rude!" Jim called.

He willed his OmniBot to unfold a collapsible shield and block the beam. The shield worked, but began to melt immediately–it wouldn't last long. Jim commanded his machine to use its own plasma cutter and return fire. He swept the beam in a short arc and sliced off the enemy's cutter, whooping in triumph as it clattered to the floor.

Hugging his OmniBot for cover, Jim leaned around it and pointed at the machine he'd just cut. Until now, he'd only commanded a robot that he was touching. Now adrenaline was flowing and he felt scared and desperate enough to try something new.

Fall, he thought.

Along with the mental command, he sent a blast of his power at the machine. In the midst of trying to shoot a tiny missile in his direction, the OmniBot lurched and tipped over onto its side. The missile fired and bounced off the floor, then off the wall, then back into the machine's own face, where it exploded.

"Two points!" Jim pumped his fist. "Wait, no, tennis rules. Thirty love! Also, who gave these things missiles?!"

He pointed to another OmniBot. This one had targeted Eli, who was busy trying to drag Kelvin's large, limp frame out of the battle zone. The machine deployed something resembling a megaphone and took aim.

Self-destruct, Jim commanded.

A red number thirty appeared on the machine's face.

Self-destruct now.

The thirty became a zero and the OmniBot ground to a halt, belching gray smoke. Jim felt its battery overload and its insides melt to slag. He whooped again, feeling impressed with himself . . . until he saw the awesome things his teammates were doing.

Natalie blocked a laser beam with one corner of a diamond shield. Reshaping the shield, she refracted the laser light so that it fired out the opposite corner to slice a second machine in half. Then she leapt at the first OmniBot and drop-kicked it with heavy stone legs, reducing it to scrap.

Zoe somersaulted to avoid a flamethrower, then dashed up the nearest wall like it was easy. Halfway up, she kicked off and tucked into a backflip and threw her arms out wide. Spikes shot from her gloves and impaled two machines, then arced with electricity that fried their insides. Still mid-air, Zoe turned inky black, and her form blurred and shifted quicker than Jim could follow. Then she was standing behind another OmniBot and it was falling to pieces.

Only one machine remained untouched. The others were occupied, leaving Jim to take care of it. He sent one more command on a wave of power. *Act like your crush just turned you down in front of everyone at the prom.*

The OmniBot spun in a frantic circle, juking in one direction and then another, before deploying the plasma cutter and blasting its own shell open. Then it turned the flamethrower on itself, melting the exposed circuitry. With a pitiful last whine, it collapsed in a heap.

Which Jim thought captured his prom experience pretty well.

Wow, how did it know what I meant? Impressive!

Zoe kicked a dead OmniBot. "So, now we have to watch out for these things, too."

"Is everyone okay?" Eli said, helping Kelvin to his feet.

"Okay? Are we *okay*?" Kelvin said, a frenzied look in his eye. "You're telling me it's not just the heroes. Now the Lighthouse itself is trying to kill us, and you ask if we're okay? This is *not* cool, man! It is a major bummer, and it is SERIOUSLY HARSHING MY CHILL! I mean–"

Zoe slapped Kelvin across the face. He stumbled back, head rattling like a bobblehead.

"Better?" Zoe said.

Hand on his heart, Kelvin sucked in a slow, deep breath. "Yes, thank you. Sorry, everyone. I haven't adjusted emotionally to being hunted for sport. It's not something–"

He froze in horror. They all did as a sound echoed down the corridor.

"Was that a lift opening?" Natalie asked.

Eli nodded. "And two voices. The heroes must be patrolling."

There was no time to hide, and opening a door would make a lot of noise. Jim saw his team come to the same conclusion. They were well and truly caught.

"I've got this," Kelvin whispered. "We're going to disappear. Everyone get flat against the wall and hold hands."

He led the way, followed by Natalie, then by Jim and Zoe. Holding hands, they pressed back against the wall as much as they could.

"If we're invisible," Zoe whispered. "We won't see an attack coming."

"Leave that to me," Eli said. "I'm the Custodian. They're not hunting me."

As if to punctuate the point, he moved to the nearest OmniBot and began gathering the wreckage into piles.

What other choice did they have? Jim shrugged. "Do it, Kelvin."

Kelvin tensed, and then everything went black. As two pairs of footsteps drew closer, Jim gave a silent prayer that these heroes wouldn't have thermal vision or super hearing. If they did, a bigger fight was coming.

They were so close, Jim felt like he could reach out and brush their clothes as they walked by. Except they must have spotted Eli, because they didn't just walk by. They stopped right next to the team.

"Custodian," a man's voice said. "What happened here?"

"Hello, Astro-Ninja," Eli said. "I didn't see it myself. OmniBots must have tried to intercept some of your prey."

"Are you certain?" a woman's voice said, cold and hard. More footsteps, as if she were moving closer to Eli. "You're not one of us. How do we know you aren't helping them?"

"Aw, leave him be, Heatsink," Astro-Ninja said. "Why would he do that?"

"An excellent question," Heatsink said. If it was possible, her voice grew even harder. "Which I would like *him* to answer."

Jim felt two hands squeezing his tighter–Natalie on the left and Zoe on the right. He was probably doing his fair share of squeezing, too. They hung in a moment of silence, waiting for Eli to decide their fate. Could they really count on him? After all, how well did they really know him?

"Well?" Heatsink pressed.

"I'm no more likely to betray the Spectrum than your–ahem–*personal rash* is likely to clear up anytime soon," Eli said.

"Wha–?" Heatsink choked. "How–you–"

Astro-Ninja roared with laughter, and Heatsink shut up altogether.

"Can I go back to my work now?" Eli said.

There was a sound like someone clapping Eli on the back.

"Best laugh I've had all week!" Astro-Ninja said. "Come on, Itchy, let's–hey wait, who's that? You, stop! Heatsink, we've got fresh meat to trap."

Two sets of footsteps dashed away, echoing into the distance. When they were gone, there was a long moment of complete silence.

"Okay," Eli said.

The blindness receded. Jim expelled a sigh of relief along with Zoe and Natalie, and stopped pressing against the wall.

Kelvin seemed perfectly at ease with the blindness, which made sense. Hiding like that must be a skill he'd practiced for years.

"Nicely done," Jim said to Kelvin.

"Thanks, pal, I'm just glad it worked."

"And thank you, Eli, for watching out for us." Natalie kissed his cheek. "You're the best."

Eli gave a gracious, embarrassed nod.

"What happened there at the end?" Zoe asked.

"Looked like a Dare contestant got separated from his team. He came around and they spotted him before he could hide."

"Poor guy. I hope he'll be okay," Kelvin said.

"Nice job with the weaponized embarrassment," Jim said to Eli. "How'd you guess she had a rash?"

"No guesses. I sense things around me, remember?"

"Ah. Well, if the Custodian gig doesn't work out, you can start a second career as the Blackmailer."

"Hey, Kelvin," Zoe said. "Why'd you tell us to hold hands? Does it help us stay invisible?"

Kelvin gave a shy grin. "Actually, I was scared, and holding hands in the dark was, um, comforting."

"Oh." Zoe turned to Jim. "Then why are we still holding hands?"

Jim looked down at their hands, and indeed, they were still intertwined. "Well, you can't be too careful. I mean, what if they come back and we're *not* holding hands. That could be the end for us."

Zoe rolled her eyes and pulled her hand away. But was that the slightest quirk of a grin?

"Time to move on," Eli said. "Follow me. There's no direct Shran tube where we're heading, so we'll have to risk taking a lift."

The team followed him around the curve of the corridor, more alert now than ever, scanning every nook for danger. As they approached the lift, he explained more of the challenge they were facing.

"You saw on the map that the Lighthouse divides into Northern and Southern sectors. I know we're in space and those terms don't truly apply, but it's colloquial. Northern Sector begins with the Torch at the top, continues down past the Spark, and includes the four levels below it. Then there's a structural divide and the Southern Sector begins."

"What's in the Southern Sector?" Zoe asked.

"There are . . . various facilities . . . but the largest portion is our training chamber. A proving ground for all Spectrum and Prism heroes. But that doesn't concern us presently. We focus now on the four levels below the Spark. Each of them has multiple paths leading to the Southern Sector, but only *one* on each level is the quickest and most direct. That's four chances to get where we're going more quickly, and hopefully with less resistance. When we get to each level, I'll explain your options, we'll recon for threats, and if possible attempt the quickest path."

"I still don't like that we're skipping the Spark," Zoe said. "Wouldn't taking their command center be a good thing, tactically?"

"And if the Spectrum lives there, we could criticize their decorating," Jim said. "They'd never recover from that."

"Quarters for all the heroes. That's like almost sixty apartments." Natalie shivered. "Can you imagine if *all* the Prisms were here right now? Facing that many corrupted heroes?"

"Yeah," Kelvin said, looking haunted.

"It'd be a bloodbath," Zoe muttered.

"True," Jim said. "Suddenly, I'm glad we're only facing fourteen powered homicidal maniacs, plus their army of murderbots. Things are looking up, and it's all thanks to positive thinking."

But then Jim realized something. If they were skipping the Spark, might they be skipping the information he needed about Summer? Or at least some clue about the green line? Suddenly, he needed more than anything to find a way onto that level.

The doors whooshed open at their approach, and the team followed Eli inside the lift.

"The lifts are the only way to reach the Spark, and they're all programmed to skip that level while carrying someone unauthorized," Eli said. "That means you. No other Dare contestants will find that level."

"Not to beat a dead horse," Jim said. "But doesn't that mean the heroes won't be hunting there?"

Glancing sidelong at Eli, Jim watched him consider the reasoning and waver. He told himself to hold back, not to press the point too eagerly. Eli himself would have to make the decision, or–

When the doors closed, the overhead lights began to flicker. Then they went dark, replaced by dim red emergency lights.

"Please tell me this is for ambience," Jim said.

Eli's expression darkened. "Not quite."

Above the keypad, a screen switched on to reveal Geometron. She wore a grin that Jim could only describe as hungry.

"Hello, kiddies," Geometron purred. "You just made a tactical error. A lethal one."

FOURTEEN

"IT'S only a matter of time before you're all dead," Geometron taunted. "All but a handful, anyway. You four can have the honor of being my next kill."

You four? Jim glanced around and noticed that Eli wasn't visible. Huh. He'd have to ask about that later, if he wasn't a crimson stain on the floor.

Zoe glared at the screen. "You trap your enemies in a box, and then you want to talk about honor?"

"It's not something I'd expect a thief to understand."

Tiny lights traced faster up and down the cybernetic half of Geometron's head. In response, heavy clanks echoed outside the lift.

Jim could feel all the safety systems shutting off, including the emergency brakes. He closed his eyes and concentrated, his power sense traveling along the utility lines that led to and from the lift.

There it is.

He found not only the control module for this lift, but the system controlling every lift on the upper levels.

"And don't you worry," Geometron said. "If any of you survive the fall, I'll be along personally to finish you off."

With a rumble, Natalie's fists became boulders. "Open this door and we'll see who goes down first."

"And I'm sure I'd get in a couple hits before you kill me," Kelvin said.

Jim had to move faster. He expanded his perception, encompassing the full array of machines that made up the lift control system.

Laughing, Geometron pressed a button, and the lift dropped into free fall.

For ten feet.

Then it screeched to a halt, emergency brakes engaged.

Geometron frowned, her little lights pulsing brighter. "What just happened?"

Jim opened his eyes. "I found the systems you turned off and turned them back on."

The hero's human eye narrowed.

"I also found where you're interfacing with the system." Jim crooked a finger and Geometron rocked back as if she'd been slapped. "Made that switch off and then on again. I imagine you'll be locked out while it reboots."

Geometron's eye unfocused, as if trying to override Jim's commands took physical effort. Finally, she gasped and her shoulders drooped in failure. Then failure turned to rage. She leaned closer to the screen.

"You," she said, pointing at Jim. "I will find you and rip your insides–"

"I also found what you're using to pipe that video in here," Jim said.

Her cybernetic eye flared red. "Don't you dare."

Jim waved. "It's been a pleasure speaking with you today. Bye-bye now."

"Oh, you little–"

The screen went dark. For a moment, only the red emergency light remained. Then the overhead strips flickered back on, revealing five people in the lift.

"Smart thinking, making me invisible," Eli said to Kelvin.

"Thanks. Figured you wouldn't want her to know you were helping us."

"Yes. The less they know, the more it gives you an advantage."

"Hey, nice work," Natalie said, playfully poking Jim. "For someone who hates heroes, you're starting to act like one."

"Aw, here I thought we were becoming friends," Jim said. "Then you go and say something so hurtful."

"She's right," Zoe said quietly. "Thank you."

"Seriously, man, that was awesome," Kelvin said.

Jim shrugged. "She's definitely going to murder me later. But hey, someone has to, right?"

"Not if I have anything to say about it." Kelvin smacked a fist into his open palm. "I mean, not me personally. I'm basically made of paper. But *me* in the collective sense."

"Unfortunately, we're stuck here," Jim said. "I have to switch everything back on slowly, one by one, or she'll regain control right away. So, where is the lift now?"

Eli brushed the doors, sensing. "The Spark's right outside."

A thrill shot through Jim. He worked to keep it from showing on his face. "Guess we have to get out here. If we can pry these doors open."

"Leave that to me," Natalie said.

She moved to the doors, crystalline hooks sprouting from her arms like oversized crowbars. Slipping the hook ends into the crack between the doors, she heaved. The doors scraped and complained, but slid open.

"Nice," Zoe said.

Natalie grinned. "Mom always said there's no problem that leverage can't solve."

"Wow," Jim said. "My mom just said lame stuff like how all the cool kids brush their teeth."

Natalie stepped through the doors first, into a small antechamber with a thick steel door on the far side. The others followed. Except for Kelvin, who not only hung back but seemed attached to the back of the lift.

"I don't know, guys. You hear those horror stories about people getting cut in half by falling elevators. Seems risky."

Natalie held out her arm and sprouted a block of dark stone. The block grew large enough to wedge itself in the opening, effectively bracing the doors open and keeping the lift from falling if the brakes failed. She beckoned to Kelvin.

"It's okay," she said. "I get nervous, too, sometimes."

Holding his breath, Kelvin dashed through the opening and pumped his fist in triumph. While he celebrated defeating an open doorway, Eli approached the ID scanner.

"Sure you want that on record?" Zoe said.

"I go everywhere. Shouldn't throw any red flags." The scanner chimed affirmative. A series of magnetic locks disengaged, and the door slid open. "Welcome to the Spark. Please don't press any mysterious buttons."

"Wow," Jim said. "No wonder my veins are buzzing like I drank static."

There were enough huge command stations here to run a small city. The cavernous dome-shaped room boasted wall-sized screens displaying data from across the world. A large circular table dominated the center, with seven chairs around it and a full-motion hologram floating above the tabletop. Smaller stations arrayed around it in concentric circles, radiating out from the center. Glass walls lined the far side, behind which sat laboratories packed with all sorts of high-tech equipment.

"I dig the mood lighting," Kelvin said.

Aside from the light coming off screens and holograms, the only illumination came from LED strips in the corners. It cast a moody glow over everything.

"That's odd," Eli said. "The Spark should have awakened automatically when I scanned in."

"This place is huge," Jim said. "We should split up, search separately."

"I'm not sure that's wise," Eli said.

"We'll cover more ground that way. Don't you want us out of here as quickly as possible?"

Plus, I can't search for Summer with you breathing down my neck, Jim added in his mind.

Eli grunted, then gave a reluctant nod. "All right."

"What are we searching for?" Zoe asked.

"Any clues about what's happening to the Spectrum," Jim said.

"And who's controlling them, and how," Eli added. "Come find me in half an hour."

The team scattered. Jim made for a small station with a screen facing a wall. As he sat and touched the controls, the screen expanded to curve around him until it encompassed most of his field of view. Despite how much he hated being here, he had to admit that was not entirely un-awesome.

He began with the usual searches for Summer Riven, the hero Lock, anything remotely related to his sister. Nothing. He expanded to include Framework, and even Anchor, since he'd died in the same battle. Still nothing. Last, he searched for anything having to do with a green line, and of course there was nothing on that either, except for . . . wait.

Jim leaned closer to the screen. An old transcript of a post-battle debriefing, where the heroes gave their accounts of what happened for the record. Apparently, this fight with an invisible villain had been going poorly. The heroes had been on the ropes, dangerously close to losing. Until one hero showed up and turned the tables.

"*The green,*" he kept saying when they asked how he'd done it. "*I followed the green.*"

The hero who'd saved them? Lord Neon.

A real clue! Jim should feel elated. But staring at this new information, he felt more alone than ever. What else was the hero keeping from him? For what purpose? Was he really trying to help, or was Jim brought here to fail?

"What's the green?" Natalie said over his shoulder.

"Gah!" Jim flinched away. "Good plan, sneaking up on someone in a tense situation."

Natalie smirked. "Good thing you didn't punch me."

"Right. Then I'd have a shattered hand to go with my heart attack." Jim swiped across the screen to clear it. "It was only a hunch. Didn't pan out. Has it been half an hour already?"

"Almost. I'm going to get Kelvin next."

"If by *get*, you mean whisper in his ear, I'm coming to watch."

They found Kelvin at a station that didn't resemble the others. It sat right next to one of the glass-enclosed labs, so maybe it was designed for some kind of research.

Kelvin stared unblinking at the screen. He stood still as a tree, one hand pressed to his sternum and the other hovering over the controls. He looked like a man frozen in time. Even stranger was his expression, which seemed . . . sad. Was the gravity of their situation hitting him now?

Natalie observed Kelvin and her playfulness dissipated. Approaching slowly, and within his field of view, she gently touched his arm.

"Hey. You okay?"

Kelvin shivered and blinked. His eyes came back into focus. "Oh, hey, guys. I . . . I found something. I think everyone should see it."

Jim's brow furrowed. "By your grave expression, I'm guessing you didn't find a secret recipe for super-brownies."

Kelvin shook his head. No jokes. Not even a smile.

Natalie volunteered to bring the others, and she returned with them quickly. Kelvin's seriousness had spread to them all. They gathered around as he presented what he'd found.

"This," he began. "Is the control panel for the Spectrum communicators."

"Whooooaaa," Natalie said.

"Good find," Zoe added.

"You examined their carrier wave, didn't you?" Eli said.

Kelvin nodded, pointing at what looked like a waveform on the screen. "This is the encrypted signal their communicators use. Note that there are two layers–one for sound and video and general data, and the other for what I'm guessing is the telepathic connection. Notice anything else? Anything unusual?"

Jim leaned in, studying the wave as it flowed across the screen in two layers, one yellow and one blue. "I'm no signal expert, aside from the crank calls I make from the bar every Friday. But this looks pretty much like what I learned in science class."

The others agreed. Kelvin watched them and gave a knowing nod, as if he still had a secret and knew they would never guess it.

"Okay," he said. "So what if I told you that this isn't from today? What if I told you it's five years old?"

Zoe shrugged. "I guess I'd ask why that matters."

"Because *this* is what it looks like today."

Kelvin tapped a key and a third wave appeared, this one an angry red edged in black. Instead of flowing along with the other two, it twisted around them and dug inside them, like thorns hooking into flesh.

The team hovered in silence while the revelation sank in.

"That seems not good." Natalie looked at Eli. "It's not good, right?"

"Looks like a recipe for the *Oops! All Villains* version of the Spectrum," Jim said. He glanced at Zoe. "No offense."

Zoe stared at the screen, her voice subdued. "I was never this kind of villain."

Eli gestured at the keyboard. "May I?"

Kelvin backed away so the Custodian could take control. His fingers were practically a blur as they flew across the keys.

"I'm attempting to trace the foreign signal, but it's slippery, unlike anything I've ever seen."

Jim watched as Eli engaged in a virtual high-speed chase with the invading signal, pursuing it literally across the planet below, ruling out potential origin points so that the possibilities slowly but surely narrowed down. He had expected to feel triumph or elation as they drew closer to their enemy's location, but as the search narrowed, he found himself filling up with dread.

Eventually, Eli stopped. The chase was over, and now that they knew the truth, Jim saw that same dread in his team's eyes.

"That can't be right," Zoe said.

"Wait, what does that mean?" Natalie asked. "It can't mean . . ."

"I'm afraid it does." Eli pointed to the proof on the screen.

Although he hadn't been able to isolate the signal's origin to a specific point, he had ruled out everywhere it *wasn't* coming from.

The only place left was the Lighthouse.

"Whoa," Jim said. "The call is coming from inside the house."

"Why not shut down this terminal?" Kelvin said. "Or smash it, even. Wouldn't that cut off the signal?"

"It doesn't work like that," Eli explained. "The system can be managed from here, but the signal is self-sustaining. The communicators are essentially their own network."

Natalie's voice quavered. "So, whoever's doing this, they're hiding somewhere in the Lighthouse? That's terrifying."

"That means we can confront them," Zoe said. "If we can find them."

Jim was about to respond when he noticed Zoe's hair gently swaying. Why would there be a breeze in this place?

She caught him looking. "What?"

"Why do you look like you're in a music video?" Jim said. He turned to Eli. "Any chance this place has wind machines to make the heroes look sexier while they work?"

Eli smirked. "I haven't gotten around to installing them yet."

Jim would have to stop later to be amazed at the fact that Eli had cracked a joke. For now, though, he tensed. "I think we may not be alone."

When the last word left his mouth, the breeze became a gust, and the sound of rushing wind filled the room.

"Move!" Natalie slammed into the team, shoving them all to the floor.

A gust of wind hit the comm terminal like a battering ram and smashed it to pieces. In its wake, a hero floated out of the shadows.

She wore a French Renaissance-era gown, with the top layers of the skirt sliced into strips that flapped in the wind blowing around her. She stared down on them with an imperious air, mouth twisted in disdain at the mere thought of being in their presence.

"Turbula," Natalie said with awe. "Mistress of the Winds."

"Cower before Turbula!" The hero lifted her upturned palms and small tornadoes spun to life over each of them. "I can smell your fear on the wind."

She had probably intended that to strike fear in her enemies. Instead, it fell to the ground like a brick. The team waited for something more, and Turbula waited while they failed to cower in terror.

Eventually, Jim broke the silence. "Well, not every catchphrase can be a winner, can it?"

Screeching, Turbula struck.

FIFTEEN

THE wind howled. Turbula might have sucked at catchphrases, but she could sling tornadoes like she was born doing it.

"I'm going to blow you away!" she taunted.

Jim grimaced, feeling physically assaulted by the pun as he leapt aside. A tornado ripped through the spot where he'd been, shredding everything in its path right down to the floor tiles. Jim wondered if the Spectrum had insurance for this place.

Next, Turbula aimed for Eli. "Traitor!"

Natalie leapt in front of Eli. "Stay behind me!"

A tower shield of gray stone sprouted from her hands, taller than she was. She jammed it into the floor and braced against it while encasing her feet in more stone. The tornado hit the shield and broke apart like . . . well, like wind hitting a big rock. Turbula attacked again, and again Natalie couldn't be moved.

Zoe popped out of the shadows. Her hands moved almost too quickly to follow, flinging darts at their enemy. But the storm winds racing around Turbula made for an effective shield, and the darts flew away before ever touching her.

Once again, Jim searched for a way to help without blowing his cover. James Cranston could turn things on and off. How would that help? He cast his eyes over the Spark, searching for . . . there. Spotlights in the ceiling, and they could get shockingly bright.

He flicked his index finger. The spotlights spun toward Turbula's face and blazed to life. Crying out, she covered her eyes and accidentally knocked herself back with a half-formed tornado.

Kelvin turned visible and pointed at Turbula. Her head disappeared, effectively blinding her.

"Yes!" He pumped his fist in triumph.

Which was the wrong move. Following his voice, Turbula unleashed a tornado and caught Kelvin full-force, flinging him through a screen with a dramatic crash. With his concentration broken, Turbula's head turned visible.

"Killing you will be a breeze!" she yelled.

"Ugh," Jim said. "Could you kill us in silence?"

Kelvin might really be hurt. Jim dashed toward his friend, but twin tornados swept by, catching him enough to lift him off his feet and toss him. Filled with the sudden adrenaline of almost dying, Jim rolled up to his knees and whirled to face his attacker. Which was a good thing, since she was pointing right at him and cooking up her next blast.

A black blur appeared near Turbula, then resolved into Zoe hanging from the ceiling and wielding a stun baton. She swung hard . . . and almost made it.

An instant before the baton struck home, Turbula turned the attack meant for Jim onto Zoe. The tornado yanked her down to the floor, then flung her up to smash through the ceiling. Then the winds stopped and Zoe dropped to the floor again. She rolled out of the way as another tornado pulverized her landing spot.

There was a scraping sound, then a boom that shook the floor. Then again, scraping and booming and shaking. Step by step, Natalie pushed closer to Turbula like a tank made of stone.

The hero turned her attention back to Natalie, her biggest threat. Spinning like a top, she loosed a barrage of tornado after tornado. Still, Natalie weathered the storm and moved inexorably forward.

She was almost within striking distance when Turbula pointed both hands at the floor and loosed a shout of exertion while slowly raising her hands toward the ceiling. A larger tornado appeared at Natalie's feet and tossed her into the air. When she flew clear of the shield, Turbula hit her square in the chest with another blast.

Natalie grew a thin layer of crystalline armor before crashing through a wall of glass. She ricocheted off a lab table, smashed through a cabinet, and tumbled to a stop on the floor, where its tiles cracked from the impact.

The buffeting winds had knocked Eli out from behind Natalie's shield. Turbula pointed at him and sneered.

"Time to *air out* our grievances!"

Jim watched her power up for an attack. All parahumans were tougher than regular people, but Eli's ability was passive. How high could his power level really be? How much punishment would someone with observation powers be able to take?

Before he could reach any conclusions, Jim found himself dashing toward Eli.

"Please, no more puns," he shouted as he ran. "For the love of God, just kill us!"

Jim shoved Eli out of the way. A split-second later, a tornado enveloped him. The force shoved him back . . . only a few steps before it dissipated.

A surge of elation raced through him. He was alive! Weird. That one must have been underpowered for Eli's sake. Maybe Turbula only wanted to kill the rest of them.

As Jim was breathing a sigh of relief, another tornado struck him full-on. Flying back, he smacked into a wall and saw stars.

"There's too many of them," Jimmy said, his voice quivering. "We're not going to make it!"

"Hey." Summer grabbed his shoulders. "James, look at me."

Sheltering behind a concrete divider while an entire gang fired bullets and energy beams at them, Jimmy regretted every moment that had led up to this. Six months of fighting crime in Highreach, working their way up from brainless thugs to full-on criminal organizations. Six months of learning and growing, of beginning to make a whispered name for themselves in hero and criminal circles.

Until tonight, when his overconfidence had led them to this. They had followed a handful of low-level underlings down into forgotten old tunnels of the train system, hoping to find a trove of illegal weapons or even a hideout.

What they had found was a trap. None of the dozens of gangsters were parahumans, but they were well-armed and more than eager to pay back the kid heroes who'd been dumb enough to nip at their ankles.

Under this barrage, their cover wouldn't last long, and neither of them were bulletproof. They were Controllers, not Smashers.

"Do you think they'll kill us?" Jimmy said.

"I think we've got a few surprises left in us." Of all things, Summer grinned. "Don't worry, Jimmy. This is our house. They just rent a room."

As Jimmy stared into Summer's eyes and focused on her words, clinging to them like a life raft, the gunfire seemed to fade into the background. Somehow, it sounded less scary now. He glanced over the barrier. There were a lot of bad guys out there, eager to take them down.

But Summer was right. They'd faced daunting odds before and survived. So why should tonight be any different?

"Hey, there he is," Summer said, brushing his cheek. "My brother, the hero. Ready to give evil a wedgie?"

He swallowed hard, squashing his fear, and nodded. "Ready when–"

An object the size of a grapefruit bounced over the barrier and rolled to a stop at their feet, red lights blinking faster and faster as it counted down. Jimmy knew that high-pitched whine. A sonic grenade!

Summer pointed at it. "Freeze."

The light stopped blinking. She must have commanded the grenade's onboard computer to seize up.

Jimmy followed suit. "Sleep."

The grenade's power source shut off.

"See?" Summer said. "They have no clue what we can really do."

And that was a good thing. This grenade may not have killed them, but the sonic blast could have deafened them and the heavy displacement of air could have broken bones. Either way, the fight would have been over.

"We're still trapped, though," Jimmy said.

"We'll figure something out."

There was a heavy industrial *thunk* of metal on concrete. The siblings glanced over the barrier, and Jimmy's stomach dropped.

"Hopefully soon," he said.

A mounted machine gun turret. The gang was bolting it to the ground and feeding an ammo chain into the monstrous thing. It must have been an antique, because it was completely mechanical. No computers or electricity, just pure old-fashioned destruction.

Okay, so maybe they *did* have a clue what Lock and Lode could do. It figured that they would pick a fight with gangsters who knew how to do their research.

"They'll punch a hole through this barrier in minutes," Jimmy said.

"Wait a second," Summer said. "You studied these old tunnels. What's underneath us?"

"Another train platform. It's active, but this late at night it's probably deserted."

"These goons only know how to use the abandoned parts, right? If we got down there, I'll bet we could escape into the active tunnel network. They'd never find us."

"Maybe, yeah, but how . . ."

Summer pointed at the sonic grenade. She raised one eyebrow–her *I've got a dangerous idea, but it's going to be fun* look.

Jimmy brightened. "You think we can do it?"

"We don't have much choice. Just tell me when you're ready."

She was right. That cannon wouldn't wait for them to strategize. Jimmy concentrated on the sonic grenade. He settled on the commands he would use, fixed them firmly in his mind, and gestured to Summer.

"Ready."

"Okay, Jimmy. Go!"

Jimmy told the grenade's battery to power back on. Then Summer told the computer to resume its countdown.

Three . . .

Two . . .

One . . .

As the grenade detonated, Jimmy exerted his will on the sonic emitter, telling it to focus all of its energy downward. The device screeched in protest as he wrestled with it, every muscle tensing until he felt like they would rip.

Just as blackness crept along the edge of his vision, the grenade obeyed. The concrete beneath them fractured and imploded, punching a hole through the floor. Clutching each other, Jimmy and Summer dropped through the hole and tumbled off the pile of concrete that collected on the platform below.

They bounced to their feet, battered and bruised but trium-phant–or alive, at least–and dashed into the shadows.

Rattling his head, Jim came back to the present.

On his left wrist, the Gauge was blinking, having some-how turned back on. He stared at the display. It showed a power level of 4.4, which was impossible. Even with his sec-ondary power–the rare one he never talked about–the condi-tions weren't right to raise his power level. He sent another *off* command and the device deactivated.

"I'm a breath of fresh air!" Turbula shouted, cackling as she loosed another tornado.

Seething, Jim spoke through gritted teeth. "I. Said. *No. PUNS.*"

No one was looking his way. This was his chance.

Two giant flat screens nearby were still receiving power. Jim grabbed them with his will and commanded them to move.

Ripping out of their mounts, the screens rose into the air and clapped together like giant hands, smashing Turbula in between. Jim pulled them apart and clapped them again. They disintegrated under the force of the blows, but left Turbula dazed.

Before she could recover, Jim commanded a power conduit to rip through the ceiling and jam into the small of her back. Screaming, Turbula careened away like a paper airplane caught in a windstorm, then crashed down hard.

"Ironically, I'm tempted to use a pun right now," Jim mut-tered as he climbed to his feet. "What a *shocking* defeat."

Turbula moaned and rolled onto her back. She prob-ably wouldn't be down for long, so they'd have to act quickly. Jim called the all-clear to his teammates, and one by one they emerged from cover.

"So," Kelvin said as they gathered. "How do we convince her to back off?"

"This one won't stop," Eli said. "She'll fight until she's dead or we are."

Zoe frowned. "I'm not killing a hero."

"I wasn't suggesting it, merely stating our situation," Eli said. "And remember, we cannot use the lift to escape."

A thought occurred to Jim. "What's below us?"

"Beneath solid floor is a layer of Shran tubes. Directly beneath those, a utility level for supporting the functions of the Spark and the apartments in the ring." Eli cleared his throat, as if debating about sharing more. "That level also has a lift. Its control system is separate from the one Geometron corrupted. However, it leads to the Southern Sector, so we would likely meet resistance."

Turbula tried to stand. "I'm the *air apparent*," she called before collapsing, unconscious.

"Ugh," Zoe said. "That's not even the right word."

Kelvin looked at Jim. "What do you have in mind?"

Jim turned to Natalie, eyebrow raised. "How do you feel about putting a hole in the Spectrum's super special hideout?"

SIXTEEN

THE floor shuddered, then shuddered again, and began to buckle under Natalie's huge stone fists. Blow by blow, it gave way until there was a hole big enough to drop through.

"There'sh a shtoooooorm brewing," Turbula said.

Jim glanced over his shoulder. The hero had awakened and risen to her knees, but was swaying half-dazed.

Encasing herself in rock from head to toe, Natalie dove into the Shran tube, where she proceeded to pummel the tube's floor until it also buckled. She dropped through it to the utility level.

"You next," Jim said to Kelvin.

Kelvin obliged and leapt after Natalie, followed by Eli. Then it was only Jim and Zoe standing over the hole while a homicidal hero tried to regather her wits enough to kill them.

"After you," Jim said.

"I'm the stronger fighter. You should go first."

"Oh, um, no thanks."

"This isn't some macho power play, is it?"

"First, no. Second, double no. Third, I would literally use you as a human shield if necessary. And fourth, if I may say so–"

"Fourth? How many do you have? You know we're trying not to die, ri–"

Zoe pitched forward with a yelp, pushed over the edge by a wheeled office printer that Jim had slowly been moving up behind her. He was surprised it still had power, given how much of it Turbula had smashed. Zoe's yelp morphed into a curse that would make a pirate blush as she plummeted through the hole.

With the team out of the room and Turbula still missing half her wits, Jim dashed over to the station where he'd been researching, which was now demolished. Kneeling among the wreckage, he sifted through the remains until he found what he'd been searching for–the hard drive where he'd saved what little he'd found. The drive was small enough to pocket without being noticed, which Jim did.

As he stood, Turbula did the same. Which was just great. She had recovered enough to spot him among the wreckage, scowl, and raise her hands.

Jim sprinted, flicking his wrists as he ran. In a twenty-foot radius around him, anything still powered by electricity–no matter how broken–leapt from where it lay and collected around him like a shield of misfit toys.

Turbula attacked. There was a rushing sound, and a clatter as her tornado sheared off the left third of Jim's improvised shield. She attacked again. Jim ducked as more chunks tore away and the shield fractured under the assault.

Just as it fell apart, Jim dropped and slid feet-first through the hole. A lethally huge tornado swept by overhead, close enough to tousle his hair.

Hands up like he was on a rollercoaster, he let himself enjoy the fall, knowing the sudden stop wasn't going to be nearly as fun.

Except, when he landed, it wasn't on a hard industrial floor. Instead, it was soft and uneven, less like the floor of a space station and more like the untouched ground deep within a forest.

Which is exactly where he was.

"Um," Jim said.

He turned, and then turned more, to examine his surroundings. Had Natalie punched so hard that the floor had become a wormhole? Because he was definitely not on the Lighthouse anymore.

It was dusk here, and the forest stretched in every direction until it faded into thick mist. Tall, broad-leaved trees rose high, interspersed with a hundred varieties of flowering greenery. The blossoms all around Jim glowed, offering multi-colored bioluminescence. In their light, he could see spongy moss covering the ground. The air teemed with the sounds of wildlife. Tiny, glowing creatures zipped to and fro, flitting from blossom to blossom.

He shivered in the damp, chilly air. "I'm in a forest right out of a fantasy movie, and I don't even get a cloak?"

A heartbeat later, a cloak settled over his shoulders.

"Nice." He stopped to consider the implications of what had just happened. "So . . . I'm in this forest, and I don't even get a billion dollars and a date with Amy Adams?" Jim waited, but nothing else happened. He shrugged. "Worth a shot."

From out of nowhere, a hand gripped his shoulder. Jim most certainly did not yelp like a frightened child, and anyone who claims otherwise is a dirty liar, but he did emit a sound of surprise, as any grown human man would naturally do, let's get that straight right now.

"It's me," Eli's voice said.

Jim saw nothing aside from the enchanted forest. "Are you a ghost? Wait, am I a ghost? Is this heaven? I always pictured it more like an airport Chili's."

"We're all caught in an illusion–an unusually strong one. I'm working on it, but it's challenging. The illusion has many layers beyond simply visual."

"Must be why it feels so real."

"Correct. With every sense engaged, your mind wants to believe."

"Should we be running or something? This feels like a trap."

"No one working for the Spectrum makes illusions quite like this, which leaves a Dare contestant. So the danger to us should be minimal."

Since they probably weren't going to die in the next thirty seconds, Jim let himself relax and resume admiring the illusion. It really did feel like a tranquil, secluded wood in some idyllic realm with elves and pixies and–

Screaming. Angry, vengeful screaming, like electrified fingernails digging into Jim's spine.

"Well, I had to know this would suck eventually," Jim said. "I mean, you let yourself enjoy a place, and the trees start screaming."

"Turbula chased us here. Must be caught in an illusion of her own. I'm trying to pierce the veil so we can . . . ah, here we go."

The forest began to waver and grow hazy, but didn't fade entirely. Still, it was enough for Turbula to come into view a dozen yards away. She faced something unseen with murderous rage.

"The goddess of winds will not suffer your evil presence!"

"You'd think someone dressed like an old French aristocrat would be super chill," Jim said. "It's never who you expect."

"DIE!"

Turbula unleashed a wave of tornadoes at the unseen thing. There was a crashing sound like expensive stuff breaking, but it seemed miles away–likely an effect of the illusion.

As she was powering up to release another blast, her rage flashed into sudden terror. Her arms dropped like wet noodles. Horrified, she shook her head in protest.

"No no no anything but that, anyone but *you*, please no!"

Wailing, Turbula spun and flew in the opposite direction like her life depended on it. She didn't make it far before stopping abruptly, as if she'd collided with an invisible wall. Her head snapped back from the impact and she collapsed, unconscious.

Jim winced. "Ouch. Someone let the wind out of her sails. Heh."

"Quiet, please," Eli said.

"You're right. No more puns. We all deserve better."

"No. Well, yes. But also I'm close to piercing the illusion." Eli squinted at something Jim couldn't see, his entire face scrunched in concentration. "There."

The illusion rolled away like a retreating fog. In place of the forest, there was a large industrial space filled with pipes and heavy wiring and all manner of mechanical doodads that Jim didn't recognize.

"Aw, man, my cloak is gone," Jim lamented.

"What cloak?" Zoe said.

Jim and Eli turned to find the rest of their team nearby, looking various levels of disoriented.

"Wow, now that was something else," Kelvin said brightly. "For a minute there, I was at a dwarven feast in this awesome underground cavern. I was the tallest guy there by a mile!"

"You got dwarves and dinner?" Natalie said, disappointed. "I was stuck in a tiny boat with some guy in, like, a Robin Hood costume, and he kept playing a guitar at me."

"At you?" Kelvin said.

"At me. He wasn't very good."

"At least you got music," Zoe said. "I was in a big pot, and a dragon was trying to decide how to cook me. At the end, he started tossing in potatoes and onions."

Kelvin looked at Jim. "What did you get?"

"Enchanted fairy forest."

"Not bad."

"It would've been better with Amy Adams and a billion dollars," Jim muttered.

"Huh?"

"Never mind."

"Everyone got their own illusions," Eli said slowly, as if chewing on the new information. "Impressive. That would take an extreme amount of focus and control. Once we're through all this, you'll make a fine hero. Any team would be fortunate to have you."

"Who are you talking to?" Zoe said.

"I'm talking to *him*." Eli reached out to the left. His hand clamped down on something invisible but solid.

"Gah! Alright, alright," a voice said. A man in his mid-thirties appeared under Eli's grip, short of stature and slight of build, with a thin mop of blonde hair. "You got me, okay?"

"What are you doing down here?" Eli said.

"Um, trying to *survive*. I'm an Illusion Controller, not a fighter. Maybe you've noticed all the heroes who want to murder us?"

"Except for seven of us, anyway," Kelvin said. He gave a little cheer. Then his face fell as if he'd just realized how not-good that was.

Natalie pointed at the newcomer. "You were the guy in my boat!"

"Yes. And I was playing a *lute*, and they're incredibly hard to master, thank you very much. Sue me for trying to create a moment."

"Well, you did take out the Slight Breeze of Death." Jim motioned toward Turbula, lying prone on the floor. "That's helpful."

The illusionist cast a rueful glance at Turbula. "Yeah, well, she had it coming. They all do. I saw two of us die before making it out of that atrium."

Hello awkward moment. He didn't realize, of course, that Eli wasn't a Dare contestant. Eli wasn't a Spectrum hero, either, but Jim got the feeling that this illusionist wouldn't feel like discussing the nuances of their situation if he found out. The others must have had similar thoughts–they shuffled uncomfortably but didn't comment.

"What's your name, son?" Eli said gently.

"Eugene. But they call me Reverie."

Eli nodded, somehow making that one gesture a greeting, a symbol of respect, and an offer of comfort. "Reverie. How about you join us? We can help each other get through this."

The man hesitated. His eyes flitted over to Natalie, and the tiniest gawky smile brushed his lips. "Yeah, okay. That'd be nice, I guess."

"Fantastic," Jim said. "When we're safe, I'll teach you the secret handshake. Spoiler alert: there's a rap break in the middle."

"We'd best be moving now," Eli said. "Time is not on our side."

Zoe looked around. "You said there was a lift on this floor, right?"

Jim studied the open space. This level wasn't actually that big, so it must be somewhere close. Although . . . that was weird. The Lighthouse was huge. Shouldn't this level be a lot bigger?

Now that he was really looking, in a few little spots where there were blinking lights or whirring machinery, Jim sensed no power. Yet, in other places where there appeared to be nothing, he saw flows of electricity. The oddities were subtle, like puzzle pieces that didn't quite line up.

You're in a place that deals in the impossible on a daily basis, he told himself.

I know, but this isn't impossible. It just doesn't make sense.

Whatever.

No, YOU whatever, brain. Shut up, I'm in charge here.

Well, that explains the pun earlier.

Eli glanced around as if confused. "There is a lift. Or . . . there should be. It was right over there. Or, wait." His eyes unfocused. "That's odd. I'm sensing–"

"Oh, right, the lift," Eugene interrupted. "Sorry, I forgot to unhide that. It's right over there."

He gestured at a tangle of pipes, which wavered and disappeared. Behind where the illusion had been, there was a red-lit alcove and the double doors of a lift like the one they had taken earlier.

"Well, if it had been a snake, it'd have bitten us," Kelvin said. "I mean, eventually, when it slithered over this way. You know what, never mind."

"Follow me," Eugene said, leading them toward the lift doors.

"Why hide the lift?" Zoe asked. "Wouldn't you want people to pass through here and leave you alone?"

"Habit, I guess," Eugene said over his shoulder. "When you only have illusion powers, your best defense is confusion. I can't throw a punch, but I *can* conjure a maze that your mind will get lost in."

Jim perked up. "Can it be a corn maze? I'm starving."

Though he made a joke, his mouth was working on autopilot while his eyes studied their surroundings. All he wanted was to find something green–an air duct, a wire assembly, he'd settle for a sewage pipe–but instead, he could only see the little bits of *wrong*. The corners where electrical flow didn't line up with machinery, or where a light strip sat six inches too far away from its power source. Though he tried to shake the growing unease, he found himself walking more slowly to look for a pattern in all the imperfections.

"So, you see it, too," Eli said quietly, so only Jim could hear. "The wrongness."

Jim nodded. "Much as I'd like to deny it, yes. I see it."

"So, Reverie, where's your team?" Natalie asked. "Are they hiding somewhere? I'd love to meet them! We can all stick together."

"They went ahead, kept moving down the levels. Everyone else had, um, more *active* powers, so we figure it'd be best if I stay here." Eugene shot Natalie a tentative smile. "Maybe now we'll catch up with them."

"I hope so!"

There was a lead weight in the pit of Jim's stomach, and it grew with every step toward the lift. Though his eyes and ears kept trying to tell him that everything was fine, his parahuman senses screamed disagreement. Something was very wrong here.

When they reached the lift, Eugene stood aside and gestured at the doors. "New friends first. I'll go in last, so I can reset some illusions before we leave. It may slow down our enemies."

"You're a stand-up guy, Eugene," Kelvin said. "Glad we made a new friend."

"Me, too."

Eugene turned his smile on Kelvin, and that's when Jim realized what was wrong with it. Only his mouth was smiling. Behind his eyes, there was hunger. His hand hovered over the call button.

Warning lights flashed in Jim's mind. He could practically hear a danger klaxon blaring, and the voices of every instinct he possessed shouting in unison.

DO NOT LET HIM PUSH THAT BUTTON.

There was no time to explain himself. Reaching toward Zoe, Jim plucked a throwing knife from her belt.

"Hey!" Zoe said.

Drawing back, Jim took aim and let the knife fly. It flipped end over end, passing over Natalie's shoulder and striking Eugene's hand.

With the blunt end.

Crap.

Eugene's hand flinched away. "Ow. What was that for?" He reached for the button again.

"No!" Eli burst forward and wrapped the illusionist in a bearhug, squeezing his arms to his sides.

"What's the deal, guys?" Kelvin said.

"You touched my knife," Zoe accused Jim.

"None of this is right," Eli said. "I can sense it."

"Me, too," Jim said. "For one thing, there's no power flowing to that lift. That's one of a dozen details he got wrong."

"Who got what wrong?" Natalie asked.

Zoe narrowed her eyes. "You're not saying . . ."

"Oh, I *am* saying it, with sprinkles and a cherry on top. This isn't real. We're still in his illusion." Jim faced Eugene. "What's on the other side of that door?"

Eugene raised his chin, defiant, and kept his mouth shut.

"I can help with that," Eli said. Eyes closed, he tilted his head toward the lift. "Nothing. Just jagged pieces of what used to be a lift, and then open space."

Kelvin's eyes widened. "You mean like *space* space?"

Eli nodded. "Our friend here was trying to bypass the safety force field and vent us into the vacuum."

Zoe stepped up to Eugene, her posture subtly turning dangerous. "Is that what happened to your team? Did you trick them? Kill them?"

Eugene didn't respond.

Natalie looked genuinely hurt. "But you're supposed to be a hero!"

Eugene sneered. "No, I'm supposed to survive. That's the game, right? The one our heroes are forcing us to play? I'm just better at it."

"Yikes," Kelvin said.

"You would do the same," Eugene accused.

"Well, you can already see we haven't," Jim replied.

After responding, he felt someone's gaze on him and turned. Zoe's eyes were burning into him. Not with anger or accusation. More like . . . but then their eyes met, and the next instant it was gone before he could identify it.

"What do we do with him?" Zoe said as if she hadn't just been caught staring. "If we leave him, he'll do this to someone else."

Eugene smirked. "I guess you'll have to kill me. If YOU CAAAAAAAAAN!"

The last words drew out, deepening until they became a rumble. His body began to transform, growing scales and wings and long, razor-sharp claws. The team fell back with cries of alarm.

127

Except for Zoe, who stood her ground while looking bored, and a bit annoyed. She flicked her wrist and a dart stuck into Eugene's neck.

With a shocked grunt, he lurched to a halt and clutched at the bolt, throwing an accusing glare at Zoe. He opened his mouth to say something, but only managed half a gurgle before his eyes rolled back.

As he collapsed, the layers of his illusion faded, leaving them in the real world. The team stood over his prone form. Zoe nudged him with her toe and they all fell back a step, tense and ready to fight. When it was apparent that he wouldn't be moving for a while, they relaxed.

"Well," Jim said. "At least he didn't use any puns."

SEVENTEEN

THE textured metal floor of the Shran tube bit into Jim's knees. He grimaced. "I haven't crawled this much since I tried absinthe. We're only going one level down, right?"

"Yes," Eli said. "The utility level was the first of four that make up the remainder of the Northern Sector. The next level down is a repair bay for ships, satellites, anything big."

"Is there another elevator there?" Kelvin said.

Eli hesitated. "In a fashion. Forgive me for not saying what we're going to find. To be honest, if you know what's ahead, you might back out."

"Can't we just skip to the third or fourth levels?" Zoe said.

"Those are no better, and they may take time we don't have. I know this is uncomfortable, but the stairwells and other regular means of traversal are likely monitored, or overrun with others trying to make their way down."

"Or psycho-killer heroes, don't forget those," Jim said.

As if on cue, the station shuddered from a distant explosion. Through all these hijinks, it was easy to forget that everyone here was fighting for their lives. At least it was unlikely that they would be attacked from behind. They'd left both Reverie and Turbula heavily sedated, blindfolded, and bound by strong cord–all provided by Zoe–and hidden in a closet.

The Shran tube curved into a downward spiral. Kelvin grunted, his head knocking against the low ceiling.

"Yeah, these are not tall-people friendly. I never guessed the Lighthouse would be so hard to get around in."

"It's probably a lot easier when you're not being hunted," Zoe observed.

"Correct," Eli said.

"Still better than sleeping in the car," Natalie muttered to herself.

In the confines of the tunnel, though, her voice bounced off metal surfaces and everyone heard her clearly. As one, the group stopped crawling, all eyes on her.

"What?" Her expression fell. "I said that out loud, didn't I?"

"Natalie," Zoe said. "Are you sleeping in your car?"

Natalie studied the floor. "Well . . . it's, uh, been a tough year, I guess. So yeah, maybe I've been living in the car a little bit." She shook her head as if trying to dismiss it. "I mean, from the day I got my powers, all I ever wanted was to become part of something like the Spectrum. Be a real hero, you know? But until that happens, trying to be a hero on your own while working minimum wage jobs, it's not like those two things play well together."

"But you have family," Zoe said. "They can't help?"

"Oh. Um, we don't exactly see eye-to-eye about what I'm trying to do." Natalie seemed on the verge of tears. She pushed them back and plastered on her best attempt at a smile. "But it's okay. Lots of people have it worse, and I know it'll be worth it one day, when I can start making a difference. Until then . . ."

She trailed off with a shrug, as if accepting that her life had to suck right now.

If pity could echo, it would be bouncing off the walls, too. In the ensuing moment of quiet, the rest of the team gazed at her with their varying brands of sympathy.

Natalie seemed to fold in on herself. "Please don't look at me like that."

How could they not? This was without doubt the saddest thing Jim had witnessed all year, and something about Natalie's determination to maintain her sunny can-do attitude made it even sadder. Jim didn't spend a lot of time thinking about the state of justice in the world, but if someone so good could be quietly struggling so hard, what did it say about humanity and the world they had built?

Well, at least Jim could honor Natalie's request and stop looking at her like that. He turned to Eli with a question he'd been wanting to ask all day. "Why are there only seven capes? I mean, if it's based on light, shouldn't there also be a black cape and a white cape?"

Eli fixed him with an incredulous, you-cannot-be-serious stare. "Now, of all times, you choose to ask that?"

Jim shrugged. "Knowing is half the battle. Cartoons taught me that."

Eli's eyes flitted from Jim to Natalie, and then he seemed to understand. Facing forward, he resumed crawling. "Black and white are not colors of the visible spectrum. Consult any seventh grader and they'll tell you that."

The silly question seemed to work, breaking the sad spell. As the team got moving again, Natalie shot him a grateful look. Jim nodded and resumed his debate with Eli.

"That's kind of splitting hairs, don't you think?"

"You mean splitting *light*," Kelvin said, then laughed at his own joke, but his laughter died when no one joined in.

"White light contains all colors of the visible spectrum," Zoe said. "Black is the absence of any reflected color."

"Hey, let's not muddy the water with actual science," Jim said. "What color is this repair bay we're crawling to?"

"Metal," Eli said flatly.

Not green, then. It had been worth asking, at least. Jim still couldn't puzzle out what Lord Neon had been talking about in that record. He had talked about "the green" as if it were something substantial, but hadn't elaborated. At least, not in the part of the report that Jim read.

He really needed to find another server room and plug in that hard drive. It would help to get a second look at the data, and hopefully he'd be able to cross-reference it with other files. Of course, first he'd have to come up with a reason why they should stop in another server room, but that was a problem for Future Jim.

As the Shran tube leveled out, they reached a T-junction. Eli led them left, where the tunnel continued for twenty yards before ending at a hatch.

"We're here." Brow furrowed, Eli placed his hand on the door. "But someone's fighting in the repair bay. I can feel two Dare contestants and one hero." He leaned closer, as if concentrating, and his face went slack. "It's Road Rash."

"That's good news, right?" Natalie said. "She seemed nice earlier."

"She really did," Kelvin said. "And it's not like a Runner can punch our heads off or anything."

Eli shot them a dark look.

"I'm guessing you disagree," Jim said.

Eli pursed his lips and looked at the ceiling, as if debating whether he should tell a group of children that the Boogeyman is real right before bedtime. He gave a resigned sigh.

"A few years back, a man marched into Piccadilly Circus in London and dropped his coat to reveal that he was strapped head-to-toe with very nasty explosives. Road Rash grabbed him and ran them both out of the city. But she didn't stop there. She ran faster and faster until the bombs shredded to pieces and the bomber's clothes disintegrated."

"Wow, impressive," Kelvin said.

"Then the bomber's skin was gone, and Road Rash kept running until friction and g-forces pulled the man apart cell by cell. When she finally stopped, all she carried was a smoldering skeleton."

Natalie shivered. Zoe stared grimly into the middle distance. Kelvin grimaced. "I should have let you finish the story."

"Don't mistake me," Eli said. "Under normal circumstances, Road Rash is a hero through and through. But in her mind, if you're willing to die in order to kill other people, you forfeit your right to exist."

Jim did his best to brush the story off, but part of him knew that mental image would be burned into his brain forever. "Wow, and that was *before* the comm network drove her mad. What's she going to be like now?"

"So," Kelvin said tentatively. "Are we moving on to the next level, or . . . ?"

On the verge of agreeing that they should move on, Jim caught a pained look that ghosted across Eli's face. There was something he wasn't sharing.

Don't ask, his survival instinct screamed. *Just keep going. You're not one of these people. You're here for Summer, so find what you need and get back to your own life.*

It was true–he wasn't one of them. But as Jim opened his mouth to advocate for leaving, he couldn't help picturing Summer here, on her hands and knees next to him in this ridiculous tunnel. He couldn't help imagining the shame on her face.

Before he could stop himself, he said, "How's the fight going in there?"

Eli looked down. "Not well."

He didn't have to explain further. Whoever was fighting Road Rash in there, if left to themselves, would eventually die.

No one said a word. They shared a look, and as they did, the mood in the tunnel shifted. Scared faces became set, determined jaws as one-by-one they willed themselves from flight to fight. Each of them nodded, silently agreeing to do this together.

"Okay, Eli." Zoe nodded toward the hatch. "Whenever you're ready."

After studying them anew, with possibly a hint of pride on his face, Eli reached for the handle. "Okay. Here we go."

"Wait, stop," Jim said.

"Jim, we're doing this." Zoe hooked her thumb over her shoulder. "You want out? Go hide in another tunnel."

Jim held up a staying hand. "No, it's not that. I have an idea."

EIGHTEEN

THE access hatch snapped shut behind Jim. There was no going back now.

Breaking into a run, he tried to observe as much detail as he could about the repair bay without slowing down. At least the size of a football field, it was a wide open space covered in gleaming brushed metal, with various sections of the floor marked to indicate what could park there. Each section was lined with all manner of shiny equipment that Jim figured must be tools for . . . fixing . . . stuff.

One rig stood out as he ran past it–something that looked like a giant robot arm growing out of the floor, with metal fingers each the size of a person. He guessed it was for clamping onto ships and holding them in place for maintenance.

The far wall was one huge panel of invisalloy facing outer space. On seeing that eternal blackness, Jim felt an instant of overwhelming vertigo and had to look away before he tripped over his own feet. He couldn't afford a mistake. If there was any chance of pulling this off, timing was key.

Set into the invisalloy was a metal chamber about twenty feet wide, with one hatch on the repair bay side and another hatch leading out into space. That was the airlock Eli talked about while they reviewed Jim's plan, with space suits and a movable platform that allowed for repairs on the exterior of the Lighthouse.

No wonder Eli hadn't wanted to tell them about this level's elevator. None of them signed up for a space walk.

That wasn't important right now. What was important were the two Dare contestants–a woman and a man–huddled back to back in the middle of the bay, bloodied and bruised with costumes torn, both looking ready to fall over. They wore matching costumes–green cassocks with iridescent vines climbing the sleeves. If they had some kind of plant-related power, this was exactly the wrong place to be.

Likely, the only thing keeping them conscious was the desperate struggle to survive the blue streak racing around them, assaulting them too quickly to be stopped or even clearly seen. Just a blur, a sound like gale force wind, and pain.

"Please, stop this!" the woman cried.

The man began, "We only wanted to–"

The bay rattled with a sonic boom. The blue streak lashed out, casting them to the floor.

The blur coalesced into the shape of a person. The windy roar faded as Road Rash skidded to a halt beside her victims. She pressed a boot down on the female hero's abdomen.

"Stop this?" She sneered. "Now, why would I do that when I'm having so. Much. Fun?"

With a malevolent grin, she reached for the woman's forehead and her hand began to vibrate like a buzz-saw. She leaned closer and closer, laughing as her victim cringed away and her friend pleaded for mercy. Jim had never seen that vibrating hand trick, but he could guess what it did. There was no time to waste.

"Oh, thank God I found you!" he called. "Please, I need a hero. Can you help me?"

Three pairs of eyes turned his way, two terrified and one annoyed. Now there really was no going back. Swallowing hard, Jim closed the distance until he stood within arm's reach of Road Rash.

"Please, I'm desperate," he told her. "I've lost my body, and I can't find it anywhere."

He nodded down at himself. Before leaving the tube, he'd asked Kelvin to make his body invisible but leave his head normal. Now he appeared to be only a floating head.

"Who are you?" Road Rash demanded.

"I am the All-Powerful Floating Head Man," Jim declared proudly, placing hands on his hips even though no one could see it. "Except, this time when I did my awesome head-floaty trick, my body ran off. No matter how much I call or offer it a tasty snack, it won't come back to me! Please, can you help me find it? I'm really desperate. I can't stress that enough."

"Dude, no," the woman on the floor warned, shaking her head. "Just walk away."

"He's a little crazy," the man on the floor said to Road Rash. "Not worth your time. You can leave him alone."

Wow. Later, Jim would have to take a moment to be impressed. Even down and defeated, they were trying to save *him*.

"You . . . lost your body?" Road Rash's eyes narrowed in suspicion. She began to turn, as if to examine the rest of the bay.

Crap, she's not buying it. Can't have her looking around. Okay, time for Plan B.

"Whoa!" Jim shouted, dancing and spinning as wildly as he could. "I'm a maniac, maaaaaaniac, and I'm dancing now but I forgot the wooooooords . . . anytime now!"

From behind Road Rash, there were six sharp bursts of air. She lurched forward, wavering as her eyes glazed over, then whirled shakily to look behind her. Half a dozen of Zoe's darts were sticking into the back of her neck–enough sedative to drop an elephant. As she turned, a sparking stun dart struck her chin.

With a rumbling sound, Natalie appeared as if stepping through an invisible curtain. Her boulder-covered fist was already swinging, and with a satisfying crunch it smashed into Road Rash's sternum. The hero fell hard and bounced off the floor like a rubber ball.

At the sound of heavy mechanical clanks, Jim moved aside. The giant robot arm came to life, piloted by Eli, and reached down to pluck Road Rash off the floor. It clamped tightly around her, finger-like appendages hoisting her into the air. Trapped in heavy metal with her feet off the floor, there was no way for her to run, even if she was conscious. Which she wasn't.

With a sigh of relief, Jim helped the other Dare contestants get back to their feet. Visible now, the team gathered around to lend support.

"I don't understand," the man said. "How did you do that?"

Grinning, Jim nodded at Kelvin.

"Ah, um," Kelvin said sheepishly. "Well, I made everyone invisible except for their eyes–you know, so they could see–and just prayed that she wouldn't spot the weird floating eyes while we set the trap."

"Thank you," said the woman. "I think you saved our lives."

"Adam," Eli pointed at the man, then at the woman. "And Helen. Correct?"

"Yeah." Adam gestured at Road Rash. "Wow. You took out one of the Spectrum."

Natalie cringed. "I feel kinda guilty about that."

"I feel kinda *not dead* about it," Jim said.

"You were trying to use the external service platform?" Eli asked.

Adam nodded. "We gambled that no one else would be willing to try it. But right before we got to the airlock, she hit us."

"Well, that's just rude," Kelvin said.

"Totally rude," Jim said. "When I was a kid, heroes had the decency to not try to murder you."

He scratched his ear. It tickled from a weird buzzing he could barely hear, like someone had switched on a motor powered by gnats.

"How could this be happening?" Helen said, on the verge of tears. "Has the Spectrum been evil all along?"

Jim prepared another quip. But as he observed these people's fear, their genuine despair, as if all their hope and faith were tearing apart, the words died on his lips.

"If it helps," he said quietly. "We think someone's controlling them. Corrupting their minds."

"It's crazy how that actually makes more sense," Adam said. "What have we gotten ourselves into?"

"We're just small-town heroes," Helen said. "We're not ready for this."

"No one's ready for *this*," Zoe said.

Jim scratched his other ear. That buzzing was getting worse. Was he imagining, or could he almost feel it on his skin? The tech in this place was too weird.

Natalie wrapped her arms around Adam and Helen and pulled them close. "We're in it together now. You're coming with us."

Adam winced. "I don't know if we can fight. She worked us over pretty good."

"Don't worry about that," Eli said. His next words cut off, and he whipped around.

Jim followed his eyes to . . . *oh, crap.*

Now he understood the buzzing. Road Rash vibrated so heavily that she was a human blur. The buzzing intensified, becoming a persistent rumble followed by a metallic groan. Impossibly, the giant clamp was struggling to contain her.

"Aw, come on," Jim lamented.

"Yeah, that's not fair," Zoe agreed heavily.

"She's one of the Spectrum for a reason," Eli said. He pointed at Adam and Helen. "You had a plan. You should stick to it. Go now."

"We can't leave you behind," Helen said.

Adam agreed. "We owe you."

Eli stepped closer, his presence seeming to grow larger as his voice turned to iron. "Go to the airlock, put on the spacesuits, and get out of here. *Now.*"

Further protests died on their lips. With reluctant nods, the two heroes thanked them again and fled to the airlock.

As the hatch sealed behind them, the vibrations rose to a deafening crescendo. The clamp ripped to pieces with a terrible metallic screech.

The next thing Jim knew, his feet were off the ground. He found himself hurtling through the air while the repair bay blurred around him. Gripping his arm with one hand, Road Rash snarled while she ran.

"You think I've never been drugged, electrocuted, beaten, and trapped before?"

"I was kinda hoping so, yeah," Jim called over the rushing wind.

Her grip tightened. "I'm going to run you to pieces."

"Can I get your autograph first? I'm a big fan."

Shouting in rage, Road Rash ran faster. Her suit reconfigured, plated segments rearranging until she was completely smooth from head to toe with no apparent edges. Zero drag. The wind slid off her like she wasn't even there.

Not so for Jim. He could feel his body stretching beyond capacity. The forces generated by her speed were literally going to disintegrate him. Black spots dotted his vision, growing larger. The air smelled like ozone. Soon he'd be unconscious.

Power . . . said his fading mind.

. . . *her suit.*

Of course. Her suit was mechanized. Those shifting plates must have a power source. Probably some kind of battery charged by her movement. Which meant electricity.

Straining, Jim reached up and clapped his free hand over the hero's faceplate. Instantly he saw it in his mind–the map of her suit and how it distributed power. With his last shred of consciousness, he grabbed the power and pulled, sucking up electricity like chocolate milk through a crazy straw.

There was a flash of light in his mind's eye. For barely a fraction of an instant, the flash was green.

Road Rash grunted, her steps faltering. As their speed decreased, everything inside Jim increased. He felt stronger and more aware, the reach of his power growing as blackness receded from his vision. While the hero stumbled, he mentally reached into her suit and turned it back on itself.

Freeze, he commanded.

Every powered suit component seized up.

Max bright, he commanded.

The hyper-advanced display in her helmet turned up high, blazing as brightly as Jim could push it.

Road Rash cried out.

Off, he commanded.

After blinding light, the display shut down completely, leaving the hero in total darkness. Then, ironically, everything seemed to happen in slow motion.

Road Rash pitched forward. Plates of her suit cracked and then shattered. As the pieces flew away, Jim wrapped both arms around the hero and clung tightly, hoping that staying close would help him survive what was about to happen. Suddenly her speed felt less crushing, as if some of her kinetic energy enveloped him, too. It all happened in less than a blink.

Then they were tumbling, flipping and bouncing repeatedly across the metal floor.

The remains of the robot arm loomed close, right in their path. Heaving with all his might, Jim spun them so that Road Rash flew in front like a battering ram, just in time to smash through the machine and send debris in all directions.

The force of the collision tore them free of each other. They flew apart, rolling separately and then sliding for what seemed like forever, until they finally scraped to a halt.

Groaning, Jim flopped over onto his back. Though he lay still, the repair bay felt like it was spinning around him like a carousel. And not the fun kind that would spin way too fast and make you throw up that time when you were twelve and had too many churros. Just a random example, of course.

Still groaning, he slowly leaned up. Road Rash lay face down a few yards away, motionless. Then, faster than he could think, she was standing above him with murderous rage in her eyes.

"You can't defeat me!" she screeched.

"I'm getting that!"

Gripping the back of Jim's head, she held up her free hand. He watched in horror as her fingers began to vibrate.

"This is my house," the hero snarled. "You just rent a room."

In Jim's mind, everything screeched to a halt. "Wha . . . what did you say?"

Road Rash drew back and prepared to strike.

A black blur flew by, and suddenly she was gone.

I'm alive!

Wait, I'm alive? Are you sure?

The blur crashed into the nearest wall, crumpling the metal. The black receded to reveal Zoe, now pinning a stunned Road Rash against the wall with one hand, while the other struck like a cobra at the hero's eyes and throat and any other soft tissue.

"Now!" Zoe called, cartwheeling out of the way.

Spikes of shimmering rock slammed into the wall around Road Rash, then quickly spread to encase her entire body up to her chin, leaving only her head exposed. Distantly, Jim thought it looked like diamond.

Darts flew from Zoe's outstretched hand, blooming across Road Rash's face, a mixed assault of electric stuns and paralyzers.

Finally the hero drooped, truly unconscious.

The repair bay fell quiet. When he was sure she wasn't moving, Jim let himself lay back down. Right now, the hard metal floor felt like the world's most luxurious futon.

What Road Rash had said, there at the end–Jim had only ever heard one person say that. Had the hero worked with Summer before . . . before whatever happened to her? Could she know something about his sister? Was she trying to give him a message?

No way, his better reasoning said. *She doesn't know who you are, and she wouldn't give you a clue right before killing you.*

Which made sense. Still, it was weird. But he had to move on. If she knew anything, she certainly wouldn't be telling him now.

Now, about that green flash you saw . . .

Oh, right. He'd been too busy almost dying to think about it, but yeah, what was that? Did it connect to this whole green line thing? So many questions. Too many.

"I'm taking a nap," he said, resuming his groan from earlier. "Let me know how this all turns out, okay?"

"Kelvin," Eli said. "Can you put a cloak around her that will stay active when we leave? And Natalie, can you reinforce that structure?"

Gathered around the hero, the three of them quietly strategized how to leave without worrying about her waking up and attacking from behind at the worst possible moment.

Which left Zoe to approach Jim and offer a helping hand. "You okay?"

"No, I'm dead. Can't you tell?"

Lips pursed, Zoe knelt beside him. "Actually, I'm kind of surprised you're *not* dead. Most people couldn't handle that kind of speed."

Despite his pain, Jim shot her a sly grin. "Oh, I can handle a lot of things."

"Are you seriously choosing this moment to flirt with me?"

Jim considered. "I was thinking about it, yeah."

"And what makes you think you have a chance?"

"Well . . . my power *is* turning things on, after all."

Zoe stared down at him with disdain. Jim waited, and slowly her mask of disapproval cracked. She laughed, and he let himself laugh with her.

"That may have been my cheesiest line yet," he said.

"*May* have been?"

"Don't hold it against me. We're in a high-stress situation. I'm off my game."

"Oh, so what does your game usually look like?"

"Same thing, except I'm standing behind my bar, which makes me seem like five percent cooler. Also, I try to seem just helpless enough that a girl feels like she can fix me."

Eli cleared his throat. "If you're both finished . . ."

"Oops. Dad caught us goofing off." Jim pointed at Zoe. "And I blame you. I'm in a vulnerable state here."

Zoe rolled her eyes. "You're an idiot."

But she was smiling as she helped him to his feet. He took that as a win.

"So," Kelvin said. "Anyone else kind of sad that we took down one of the Spectrum, but probably won't ever get to tell anyone about it?"

"But we saved Helen and Adam," Natalie said brightly.

"True," Kelvin agreed, sounding encouraged.

As a group, they gazed at each other. Jim could feel them all taking new stock of the situation they were in. Yes, it was dire and horrible and other adjectives, and they faced monumental odds, but somehow these misfit strangers had found a way to work together as a halfway functional team. Understanding passed between them all, and they seemed to stand a little taller.

"Maybe we can do this after all," Zoe said. "Beat the game, save everyone. If we work together."

"I don't have anywhere else to be." Jim shrugged. "Let's give evil a wedgie."

"What?" Natalie said.

"Nothing. Eli, what's next?"

Eli wore a proud smile, like a parent watching their child take its first steps. "Okay. If we play our cards right, this next move may be the last one we need. It starts with–"

A loud tone blared from speakers in the ceiling, echoing across the repair bay. On every wall, display screens switched on.

"What's that?" Natalie said.

A haunted look passed over Eli's face. "Station-wide alert."

The screens filled with Geometron's face. "Hello, kiddies. We interrupt your regularly scheduled mayhem to add a little twist to the game."

She stepped back, giving the camera a wide view. Three Dare contestants stood on the atrium stage with her, chained to stone pillars and wrapped in power cables, mortal terror on their faces.

"Do you *really* want to be a hero?" Geometron stared into the camera, and her fake plastic smile turned dark. "Time to prove it."

NINETEEN

"**YOU** all want to save the world, but you don't know the cost. Not really," Geometron said. "The cost is pain."

"Is this from the mind control?" Zoe said. "Or was she always crazy?"

"I'm guessing a little from Column A, a little from Column B," Jim replied.

They looked at Eli, who gave a reluctant nod.

"In thirty minutes, this cute little baby super team will die. It will hurt." Geometron pulled the camera closer until her glowing red eye filled half the screen. "Unless someone rescues them. If anyone has the guts to try. If you do, and if you get past me, I will concede and let you escape. If not . . ."

Holding the camera at arm's length now, Geometron circled behind one of the Dare contestants and placed her chin on the young hero's shoulder.

"What's your name, sweetie?" she purred.

"H-Haley," the girl said, her voice quivering in terror. A tear slid past her gold domino mask and down her cheek.

"My God," Kelvin said, sounding haunted. "She can't be more than sixteen."

"No no no, silly, your *hero* name. Say it." Geometron waited, but her prey was trying to hold back more tears and couldn't speak. "SAY IT."

"Kalliope!" the girl choked out.

"How cute. Isn't she adorable, all grown up in her little gold costume?" Geometron turned to whisper into Haley's ear, but loud enough for the camera to pick up. "Sweet Kalliope, if no one comes to rescue you, or if they try and fail, you will die . . . and I will make them listen to your screams." She faced the camera again. "That's the game now. Ready? *Go.*"

The screen turned black and a red countdown clock appeared–30:00 in large block numbers.

29:59

29:58

"It's a trap," Zoe said. "It has to be."

"Yes," Eli said. "Geometron is too calculating to take chances. She must believe she cannot lose."

"But-but does that even matter?" Natalie said. "It doesn't change what we have to do, right?"

"No way, sister," Kelvin said. "With lives at stake, the odds shouldn't matter."

"They do when these aren't the only lives we're playing for," Zoe said. "What about everyone else they're hunting?"

"Agreed," Eli said. "If we press forward, if we complete our objective, how many more might we save?"

"Sacrifice actual lives to save theoretical ones?" Kelvin said. "I don't know if I can stomach that."

"I know I can't," Natalie said.

No one yelled. They weren't even really arguing. Jim knew they all wanted the same thing, ultimately. But right now they felt lost, and that undertone of desperation laced through every word, every pained expression.

What would he choose if it were up to him?

"Jim?" Kelvin said. "Uh, Jim?"

"Hey." Zoe thumped his arm. "You with us?"

Jim flinched, snapping out of his thought spiral. Only then did he see them all looking to him. Only then did he realize the team was split, two for one plan and two for the other.

"Let me guess. I'm the tie breaker?" He sighed. Then he chuckled at the irony. "You know, in high school, I quit the debate team after one day, and we only debated what was the superior snack food."

"Twenty-nine minutes, Jim," Eli said. "We need to make a decision."

"Right." Jim rubbed his temples, eyes closed. "A decision."

"Stay away!" Kickback shouted. "Don't come any closer, Lock!"

"Okay okay." Summer held out an open palm, a calming gesture. "Whatever you want. Just . . . don't jump. Stay right there. Can you do that for me?" With her other hand, she waved at Jimmy. "Lode, back off a bit."

Jimmy complied. Standing behind his sister on the roof of a fifty-story building, he watched as Kickback scooted forward on the ledge. The man was staring over the side now. One step and it would be over.

"Alright." The criminal mopped his sweaty brow. "Alright, now st-st-stay back or I'll jump!"

Inside, Jimmy's anger blazed. Maybe this guy *should* jump. "After what you did–"

He cut off as Summer shot him a look. She waved him back again, the message clear. She would handle this.

"You're upset," she said gently, taking one tentative step toward the criminal, as if he were a wild animal. "I don't blame you."

"I said stay back! I'm a dangerous man. I hurt people, and I'll hurt you, too!"

"I don't think you will."

Kickback grimaced, scrubbing hands through his thinning brown hair. "I hurt a *lotta* people today."

"I know," Summer said. "But I also know you didn't mean to."

Kickback looked at her with a start.

"Your device's onboard computer," she explained. "I got a read on it before things went wrong. I know what you were trying to do. It just turned out badly."

The criminal struggled to keep his mask of defiance. Jimmy watched as it cracked and then crumbled, and Kickback's face became pure agony.

"I didn't," he sobbed. "I didn't wanna hurt no one. I only wanted the money, I swear!"

"I know," Summer said in that same gentle voice. She took another step forward. "I know you did, Louis. When the police get here, I'll tell them, and they'll listen."

"It don't matter," Kickback said, swiping tears off his cheeks only to have them replaced by more. He leaned over the edge as if the void were calling, beckoning him to jump. "My life is over now. It *should* be over."

"I disagree."

"I'm the enemy, Lock. Why you tryin' to help me?"

"I guess, technically, yes. We're on opposite sides. But I've seen you walk away from a score when it would've hurt someone. In this world, there are criminals and there are *villains*, and Louis, you are not a villain. You never were."

"How can you know that? Didn't I just do what villains do? Doesn't that prove I'm no good?"

"A villain doesn't care who they hurt. Some even enjoy it." Summer stepped closer. "But look at you now, Louis. Look how you're suffering. That's why I'm trying to save you. Because someone who can regret what they've done and want to do better–that's the kind of person the world needs. That's the kind of person we can't afford to lose."

Eyes squeezed shut, Kickback shook his head as if refusing to believe her. He slid forward on the ledge, his toes hanging over empty air now.

Summer raised her voice, trying to hold his attention. "Who knows, Louis? One day, the world may need you to save it."

"It . . . it may need *me*? How?"

"I don't know. But when that day comes, I need you to be there with me." She was close enough to touch him now, holding out her hand. "We can't afford to lose good people from this world. Not even one. Please, Louis."

The grief-stricken criminal seemed to waver. He teetered, looming over the edge. Summer leaned in, silently pleading for him to make the right choice.

Finally, with a cry, Kickback took her hand and stepped off the ledge. He fell to his knees, a mass of tears, while the young hero who'd saved her life wrapped her arms around him, offering a ray of hope.

"Jim?" Eli prompted.

With a wistful smile, Jim stared into the middle distance, still seeing the memory of his sister. "If Summer were here, she'd say we can't afford to lose even one good person. The world may need them someday."

"Um, who's Summer?" Natalie said.

Somehow, this old life was pulling him back in. All he'd wanted was to run his crumbling old bar and be left alone. Then all he'd wanted was to find the truth about Summer and be left alone. Now, as obstacles piled up, as more and more people needed saving, he felt the hunt for the green line slipping ever farther away.

Jim sighed. "Sometimes I wish I cared as little as I pretend to."

"Hey." Kelvin put a hand on his shoulder. "You okay, buddy?"

Jim blinked. Everyone waited for him. There were twenty-eight minutes and forty-five seconds left.

"We need to go back," he said. "Those lives aren't hypothetical, and if there's even a chance . . ."

He trailed off, but half a statement seemed to be enough.

Eli nodded. "Okay, Jim. Let's get it done."

The rest followed suit, and just like that, they were a team again.

Jim chuckled. "And hey, if we die up there, at least we'll have a nice view."

"Silver lining, I dig it," Kelvin said.

"Great decision, Jim," Natalie said, beaming at him.

Zoe said nothing. But when Jim glanced at her, she was studying him as if she'd never seen him before. When their eyes met, she looked away.

"Let's retrace our path through the tubes," Eli said. "It'll get us moving in the right direction, and we can make plans on the way."

It was as good a suicide plan as any, so they all followed him back to the hatch. Caught up in his own thoughts, Jim hadn't noticed that Zoe was walking beside him until she spoke.

"So, did you lose the debate?" she asked. "Is that why you quit?"

Jim flashed a grin. "No, I won. Twinkies all day!"

TWENTY

UP they went, back through the twisting service tubes and onto the utility level beneath the Spark. They took a brief detour to make sure Reverie, aka Eugene the Murdering Illusionist, was still trussed and sleeping like a baby beside Turbula.

They found only Reverie.

"Well," Kelvin said. "That's mildly disturbing."

"If anyone feels a breeze, start screaming," Jim said.

"Won't that give us away?" Natalie said.

"Yeah, but it'll drown out her puns, which frankly hurt a lot worse than the tornadoes."

Zoe shut the door on Eugene. "This changes nothing."

"Agreed," Eli said. "We keep moving."

So they did, ascending back up through the hole in the ceiling, into the half-smashed remains of the command center. Jim observed the expensive debris as they picked their way toward the lift.

"I hope the Spectrum has insurance," he said.

He also felt a small, rectangular object pressing against his thigh, a reminder of the hard drive he'd pocketed. The clues he needed–to the green line and ultimately to Summer–might just be buried somewhere inside it. If he could steal a few minutes alone with a computer.

Focus, he thought, forcing his mind back to the mission. *For once this decade, think about someone else.*

But . . . it's Summer, another part of him said.

He shook off the lingering thought as they stopped at the lift, where a flick of his fingers and a nudge from his will was all it took to reactivate the mechanism. Interesting. His insides were still buzzing. Must be from the power he absorbed from Road Rash's suit. Now, that was some high-quality electricity.

"Wow, you're getting good at that," Natalie marveled as the doors slid open.

"Yeah, evil better watch out if it has to change floors," Jim said.

"How do we know Geometron isn't still watching this thing?" Zoe asked.

"I imagine her attention is focused on the Torch now," Eli said.

It made sense, though Jim kept his senses tuned outward as they stepped into the lift. He tensed as the doors closed, but the only thing that followed was a gentle upward motion.

"So," Jim said to Zoe as the car rose. "Do you like pineapple?"

She shot him a puzzled look. "Um, I guess. Why?"

With a ding, the doors opened on the docking bay level.

"To be continued," Jim said.

They stepped into the circular hallway and followed Eli around the curve, back toward the next access hatch and another exciting trip through the Shran tubes. Not far to go now.

At the head of the group, Kelvin slowed as the doors to the Reliquary rounded into view. "Hey, didn't we shut these on the way out?"

He was right. The doors were open now. Peering inside, Jim saw that someone had smashed at least a dozen display cases. Whatever had been inside them was gone.

He whistled. "Guess we weren't the last to find this place."

"Whoever came after," Eli said. "They made unwise choices."

"Unwise, or desperate?" Zoe said. "Looking for anything that might help them survive."

Eli acquiesced. "Perhaps I judged too harshly."

"Gotta admit, they're tempting," Kelvin said. "I'd love to take the Kettle for a spin. We'd make quite an entrance, driving a huge armored car to meet Geometron."

"If you can fit that in the elevator, you earned it," Jim said.

"This isn't a shopping spree," Eli said. "Keep moving."

Zoe tensed. "Wait. My gear is picking up footsteps."

Eli's eyes unfocused. "She's right. It's . . ." He trailed off, likely immersing himself in environmental sensations, then snapped back to the moment. "Everyone hide. *Now.*"

"I can make us invisible," Kelvin offered.

"It won't work. Clarion will still hear you."

"Clarion?" Natalie said. "Oh, no."

Eli veered into the Reliquary. "Everyone hide in the Kettle."

He led them to the back of the transport, where he opened an armored hatch and beckoned them to pile in. Pile in they did, a tangle of arms and legs and torsos squeezing together to lie flat on the floor and stay out of sight.

"Now I know what a sardine feels like," Kelvin whispered.

Jim couldn't bring himself to agree. In their rush to get out of sight, he'd ended up lying face to face with Zoe, scrunched together by circumstance and the need to survive. It was a tough job, but he was focused and determined enough to stick with it.

"He's close by," Eli said. "Do not move."

Zoe looked in every direction except at Jim, which was impressive considering their noses were almost touching.

"Pineapple's my favorite food," he whispered.

"What?"

"It's the ultimate snack–sweet, tangy, juicy–yet it goes with any dinner course, from appetizer to dessert. Except pizza, as I am not a psychopath."

Zoe nodded, but didn't respond.

"What's yours?"

"What's my what?"

"Your favorite food."

"You're seriously asking me this now?"

"How else am I supposed to get to know you? Help me out here."

"We could die at any moment."

Jim sighed with mock drama. "I'd die a lot happier knowing your favorite food."

Zoe looked away again, lips pursed. Was she doing that because she was annoyed, or trying not to smile? To be fair, maybe Jim had gotten a bit too weird with this one.

Zoe huffed. But then her expression softened, and she met his eye. "Chicken biscuit crackers."

Jim grinned. "Tell me your favorite color, and this could almost qualify as a first–"

"Enough," Eli snapped. "He's here."

Jim could hear it now. Footsteps and another sound, a soft clacking. Step-step-clack. Step-step-clack. The clack must be Clarion's staff, the device through which he channeled sound and created his constructs out of sound waves. They were drawing closer.

And the closer they drew, the more everyone could hear something else.

"Dun-dun-dun-*dun*, dun-dun-dun-*dun*, dun-dun-dun-*du-uuuuuuunnnn*. Clarion, cleverest and most respected of the Spectrum, prowled through the Reliquary in search of his prey."

Was he . . . ?

"I'll find my prey, *he said handsomely*, and they will pay." The step-step-clacking sound followed the deep, overly dramatic voice. "For evil must hear the clarion call of justice."

Was he actually . . . singing his own theme song and narrating his own heroic exploits?

"They thought they could run from him, hide from him," Clarion growled. "But sound never lies."

Jim bit down hard on his lip, calling on every shred of will power to keep from laughing. At the end of his nose, Zoe trembled with silent laughter.

The voice and the step-step-clack turned in their direction.

"The sound was everything, and Clarion *was* sound."

With effort, Jim buried his mirth. He saw Zoe physically recollect herself and do the same. Ridiculous or not, Clarion wielded power that all of them should fear, and he'd survived as a Spectrum hero for years.

Step-step-clack. Step-step-clack. He must be close enough to reach out and touch.

Don't just lay there, Jim's brain chided. *Do something, man!*

Okay, fine, geez. Wait, is it "lay there" or "lie there"?

Sigh.

Fine, never mind.

A distraction. That's all he could think to try. Some bit of tech or machinery he could turn on. Hopefully, it would make enough noise to lure Clarion away.

Jim stretched his senses outward, searching for the loudest thing he could manipulate while staying perfectly still. That bank of lights–could he overload them enough to make a loud pop? Clarion seemed like the type who'd be distracted by sparkles. Or his own reflection. The lights were worth a try, at least, or–

His concentration broke, interrupted by a loud blast of music. Coming from somewhere on their level, *When A Man Loves A Woman* echoed down the donut-shaped corridor and into the Reliquary.

"Ugh. The remake?" Clarion's voice dripped with disgust. "No one makes the Master of Sound listen to Michael Bolton!"

The step-step-clacking rushed toward the Reliquary doors and into the hallway, carried on waves of self-narration.

"Clarion bolted out of the room. The scent of evil was stronger than ever, and he had a nose for justice . . ."

The voice faded away as he chased down the music. The team released a collective sigh.

"Aside from nearly dying," Jim said. "That was the greatest thing I've ever witnessed. I want to hear him narrate normal stuff, like taking a shower or doing the dishes."

"Or brushing his teeth," Zoe said, a glint of mirth in her eye. "Do you think he'd talk around the toothbrush?"

"I think my life won't be complete until I find out."

"We should be safe to move." Eli opened the hatch.

When they had piled out, Kelvin patted Jim's shoulder. "Nice move with the music. Where'd you find a stereo to turn on?"

Jim held up his hands. "Don't look at me."

With a satisfied little smile, Eli held up the whistle he'd taken from this very room. "Echo Chamber. I told you it might come in handy. Blow into it, and you can do all sorts of things with sound. One of Clarion's many, *many* arch-nemeses used to carry it."

"Alright, Eli!" Kelvin cheered, raising his hand. "Hero five, up top."

Eli hesitated, then awkwardly tapped Kelvin's hand, looking as if he hoped they would all pretend it hadn't happened. "Only, uh, doing my part. Shall we continue?"

Once more, they followed him out of the Reliquary, but aimed in the opposite direction this time. The access hatch awaited.

Jim began to narrate. "Slyly, Jim slipped out of the Reliquary with his faithful companions."

Rolling her eyes, Zoe pushed him away. This time, she was definitely hiding a smile.

"Jim hoped that evil was hungry," he continued. "Because they were about to feed it a knuckle sandwich with lettuce, pickles, and a healthy smear of *justice*."

TWENTY ONE

ELI disengaged the lock, but only opened the hatch an inch. The team scrunched inside the tube, listening for sounds that might suggest an ambush. Jim had no idea what an ambush would sound like, but still, it didn't hurt to check.

"Dead silent, and I don't sense anyone in the immediate area," Eli said.

Natalie groaned. "Please don't say *dead*."

"We're two levels below the Torch now," Eli continued. "I suggest we take the stairwell up the remaining flights. If we hurry, we should avoid notice. Hopefully."

No one else had a better plan, so they agreed and slipped through the hatch. With Eli in the lead, they crept up the first flight of stairs, heads on a swivel, flinching at the slightest noise or stray puff of air.

Halfway up this flight of stairs, Kelvin flinched. "Whoa!"

Jim spun, preparing to slap someone to death if they came too close. The other teammates reacted with their own versions of fight or flight.

Kelvin clapped hands over his mouth and scrunched his body, as if he wanted to implode and disappear from embarrassment.

"Sorry," he said through his fingers. "My shirt tag scratched my neck, and I thought a hero was going to murder me."

Jim dropped his hands, working hard not to sigh with relief. "See, that's why I plan to fight crime naked. No distracting tags, and it's extra breezy in the summer."

"Want me to cut the tag out?" Zoe flourished her fingers and a slim dagger appeared in her grip.

"I'm fine now, thanks." Kelvin puffed a deep breath and slapped his chest. "Yeah, all good."

Eli rolled his eyes. "Moving on."

They ascended, completing this flight of stairs and pausing on the next floor long enough to confirm they were still alone. One more flight up and they'd be on the atrium level. Then things would get interesting.

But in that brief pause, Jim spotted it. The green door. The one leading to the little server room where they'd found Eli. There were terminals in there, easily accessible and configured to process the data on Jim's stolen drive.

His pocket felt heavier now, as if the little rectangle hidden there had its own gravity that was pulling him toward the room. With the possibility of learning about Summer so close, his baser instincts roared back to life and grabbed the wheel.

Keep moving, his better sense yelled. *Those hostages only have seventeen minutes.*

But it's Summer, another voice insisted. A voice that he recognized now as teenage Jimmy Riven. *Summer would risk everything–anything–for us.*

He rattled his head, trying to push that voice into the background. But then . . .

What if she really is alive? What if she needs help? What if we could save her?

For a split second, he *was* Jimmy Riven again, crying over his sister's grave, wishing he could trade literally anything in this universe for one chance to go back and save her.

As the moment passed, Jimmy dissipated, leaving Jim in his place–but a Jim who remembered, now more than ever, why he was here. Only days ago, this dumb hero life was worlds away, and he preferred it that way. If he'd chosen not to come, Geometron's hostages would still be where they were, and someone else would have to save them. Couldn't Jim take two minutes to search for a fallen hero who deserved better than what life had given her?

Eli stepped onto the next flight of stairs.

"Wait. I have an idea." Jim pointed his thumb toward the green door. "Give me a minute and I can rig up a better attack on the Torch."

"Is there time for that?" Zoe asked.

"Explain, Jim," Eli said.

"If I'm closer to the computers, I can use my power to manipulate systems in the Torch itself. Soften up the target before we strike."

Eli looked doubtful, glancing significantly at the countdown clock on the nearest display. "Is it really worth the delay?"

Jim couldn't risk them spending more time debating. He stepped away from the group, heading toward the green door.

"Just trust me," he said over his shoulder. "Be right back."

As soon as the green door closed behind him, he sprang into action. Two open terminals. Pick one. Butt in chair. Hard drive in hand. Plug it in. Wave Lord Neon's phone to bypass the login screen.

Only twenty seconds, and he already had Lord Neon's old mission transcript open, with the computer cross-referencing every term in the record with every file it could dig up. For good measure, he brought up Summer's basic file and folded its data points into the search. Maybe Summer's file and Lord Neon's transcript combined could bring up results he wouldn't find with either one alone.

Results scrolled down the screen . . .

Come on, come on, give me something I haven't seen. Anything about the green or the green line. A hint about Summer and what really happened.

The results were all random. Even the computer was grasping at straws. He clenched his fists.

Please. Show me this whole stupid mission wasn't for–

The green door opened. Jim looked up with a start.

"Hey, buddy," Kelvin said. "We've gotta get moving or– what is that?"

His eyes had locked onto the computer screen, which prominently and unmistakably displayed Summer's file, including her name and photograph.

Jim faltered. "Um . . ."

Before he could come up with a good explanation, the rest of the team crowded in the doorway.

"You're searching for someone? I thought you were doing something about Geometron?" Natalie pointed at the screen. "Hey, you said the name Summer earlier. Is that her?"

"Jim, what's going on here?" Zoe said.

Eli shook his head, disappointed, as if he'd understood immediately what was happening.

Jim could talk himself out of this. There might be a way to half-truth his way around what they'd seen. But . . .

Hanging his head, he backed away from the terminal. "Look, I, um. I haven't been totally honest with you. About me, and some other things. See, I'm . . . I'm not who you–"

A sudden cacophony drowned out his next words–the sound of rushing wind, as if a storm had appeared out in the hall. The team turned as a tornado hit, throwing them through the doorway and into the server room. They tumbled in a heap.

A voice echoed from outside the door. "Who's going to die today? The answer is blowin' in the wind!"

Jim didn't have time to lament another horrible attempt at a catchphrase. Leaping at the door, he grabbed it with both hands and swung with all his might against the wind.

"Maybe talking's not your thing!" he shouted just before the door slammed shut. "Turbula's out there."

"Oh, is she really?" Zoe snapped. "I couldn't tell."

"And she's not alone." Jim held up two fingers. "I saw two more with her. A man in a black spacesuit thing, and a woman in a leotard, orange on top and fading to white at her boots."

"Astro-Ninja and Heatsink," Eli said, helping his companions to their feet. He fixed Jim with a hard stare. "Congratulations, Jim. We slowed down long enough for Geometron to spring a trap."

"Do we know this was a trap?" Kelvin said.

Just then, the room's wall display switched on to reveal Geometron looking far too satisfied.

"So, you took the bait and came back," she said. "No, don't try to hide, Eli. It's too late for that. Did you honestly think I wouldn't be watching for someone to come my way? Now you get to sit there, listening while Kalliope and her little friends die. Don't worry, you only have to wait fourteen minutes."

"Geometron." Eli paused, as if gathering himself. "Azita. Please don't do this. You don't *have* to do this."

The hero cocked her head, as if confused. "Uh, yeah, I know. But it's fun."

"Water slides are fun," Jim said. "This is just messed up."

"You know this room won't hold us!" Natalie cried.

"Feel free to step through the door anytime. My friends will give you a grand welcome."

Geometron waved. The screen went black, only showing the countdown.

13:49

13:48

13:47

"Oh God." Kelvin scrubbed hands through his hair. "We *are* trapped."

Zoe turned to Eli. "Please tell me there's a way out of this room."

"Yes. The *door.*"

"No other way at all?"

"This isn't the house from *Clue*, Miss Blake. Not every room has a secret passage."

"There's another way out of this," Jim said, forcing confidence into his voice. "Together, we can figure it out."

Zoe seethed. "Says the guy who lied and got us all trapped in here."

Jim looked at the floor, feeling gutted. "It's pretty obvious now that I'm not really a hero. I didn't come here because I wanted to join. I came for . . ."

Catching an odd motion over Zoe's shoulder, Jim trailed off. His eyes narrowed. While the rest of them lamented their situation, Kelvin had quietly sidled up to Jim's computer. Instead of typing, though, he held his right hand toward a data port. The tip of his index finger separated into tiny segments and peeled open to reveal a plug. A data interface.

"Uh, Kelvin?" Jim asked. "Whatcha doing?"

Kelvin looked haunted. "If there's really no way out . . . I'm so sorry."

He plugged his finger into the computer, and the screen went haywire.

"Stop that!" Eli cried. "What are you doing?"

"Completing my mission." A tear trailed down Kelvin's face. "My real mission."

TWENTY TWO

"YOU'RE going to hate me now. I wish we could've been friends for real," Kelvin said, his voice thick with emotion. "For what it's worth, I didn't volunteer for this. I didn't have a choice."

The computer screen changed almost too quickly for the eye to follow, flickers of network maps and file trees and cascading lines of code. The machine's internal fan switched on with a labored whine, as if heat was building too quickly to vent.

"Unplug yourself!" Natalie said.

"I can't! He told me if I stop before it's finished, this would get much worse."

"Who told you, Kelvin?" Eli said. "What is he making you do?"

Kelvin looked at them with the face of a man walking to his own gallows. "The Chaos Merchant."

Everyone froze, jaws dropping.

"The Chaos Merchant," Eli said. "He's making you steal a file? Why?"

"I made mistakes, so many mistakes. Got in trouble with the law. Someone–" He cut off with a sob. "Someone came to me. Offered to make it go away. I didn't know who he worked for, I swear. Not until it was too late."

"What is he making you steal?" Eli said.

"No," Kelvin said. "Not steal."

With a soft beep, the screen stopped moving. Then every-thing cleared, dispersing as if Kelvin had unzipped the machine and now it was zipping back up. In seconds, the screen was blank except for one message, which pulsed for an instant and then disappeared.

FILE UPLOADED

"Wait, you didn't steal something, you *added*?" Zoe said, incredulous.

"Kelvin, how could you?" Natalie wailed.

"What was that?" Eli demanded. "What did you hide on our network? *Where* did you hide it?"

"I don't know. They didn't tell me anything." Unplugging, Kelvin waited for his fingertip to reform, then rubbed his palms over his face as if he wished he could scrape this moment out of his brain. "I only knew this was supposed to be my last job. They said it would settle my debt."

Eli looked dubious. "Your debt to the Chaos Merchant?"

Deflating, Kelvin nodded. "For getting me out of trouble. He gave me a cover identity, somehow made sure I got invited for the Dare. He had all this cyber-stuff put inside me so I could deliver . . . whatever that was."

So, that was what Jim felt when he'd shaken Kelvin's hand. Now he could only watch all of this happen as if it were a movie, powerless to change the outcome. All the while, his gut twisted and writhed. This was his fault, too. If he'd kept moving, if he'd put the others first, this might not have happened.

Kelvin looked at him. "Is that why you're here, Jim? It can't be witness protection. Did the Chaos Merchant send you, too? Give you that name?"

Great. Thanks, Kelvin.

Three sets of accusing eyes turned on Jim now.

"James Cranston isn't your real name?" Zoe said, her voice dangerously quiet.

Jim sighed. He did that a lot lately. "James is. Cranston isn't. But I'm not here because of the Chaos Merchant. I was sent here by . . ." Should he reveal this to anyone? Did it even matter anymore? ". . . by Lord Neon."

"I-I don't understand," Natalie said. "Why would a Spectrum hero–"

Kelvin hissed, clutching his torso. "It hurts. Something's burning inside me. It's burning!"

Jim could feel it now. Inside Kelvin, something battery-powered had switched itself on. Its power was cycling now, and building second-by-second.

Kelvin's hiss grew into a cry of pain. "Oh God, what's happening?"

Eli knew what was happening, just as Jim did. They locked eyes, silently confirming it for each other. But Jim could barely bring himself to say the words.

"Kelvin. They put a bomb inside you."

"What?!" Kelvin cried.

"Everyone back up," Eli said. "Get as far away as you can. Natalie, we need a shield." He looked to Kelvin. "You poor fool. Did you really think the Chaos Merchant gives anyone a way out?"

"Do something!" Natalie cried. "Help him!"

"I can't." Eli shook his head sadly. "I'm sorry, son."

Kelvin was sweating now, as if heating up from the inside. He yanked desperately at his jumpsuit, unsnapped the torso and clawed at his undershirt until it ripped open. His bare chest revealed hundreds of stitching scars. In his chest, beneath the skin, something was glowing. And it was getting brighter.

He dropped to his knees, moaning in agony. "I don't want to die. Not like this."

"Make a shield *now*," Eli commanded Natalie.

"No, wait," Jim said.

"Jim," Eli warned.

"Just wait!"

It was all too much. A whirlwind of awfulness with Jim at the center, lost for what to do. All he'd wanted was to find Summer, and now this sad fake wannabe hero who'd sort of become his friend was . . .

Jim didn't feel himself moving. He was just there, on his knees and facing Kelvin. He reached out, one hand on Kelvin's shoulder to steady him, the other an open palm against the glow in his chest.

"Natalie, get ready with that shield," he said, and drew a deep breath. "Kelvin, make me invisible. Then do not move."

In too much pain to speak, Kelvin could only nod. He waved his hand, and the world went black.

Jim's parahuman senses roared to life, "vision" springing up in his mind's eye, a world made of streaming blue-white energy. He trained all his focus on the complex network of power embedded in Kelvin's body.

It was unlike any he'd ever seen—a system built specifically to deliver the file, then vaporize itself and everything nearby. A battery in Kelvin's chest, no bigger than a poker chip, powered the whole system. This thing could run a building by itself, and once it cycled up to maximum output, the final command would trigger.

Jim only had seconds. Teeth gritted, he mustered all his power and flung it out wide. Then he commanded it to snap back, wrapping around Kelvin like a vacuum seal, sinking under his skin and through his bones.

It surrounded the battery first, then all the power lines snaking through Kelvin's body. Destructive energy would burst down his extremities if it wasn't contained. The entire system, every last centimeter—Jim coated all of it in overlapping layer upon layer of his own electrokinetic power. Then he squeezed and held on tight and muttered a prayer.

The battery triggered.

It felt like fire racing through Jim's veins. He cried out, his whole body shaking, refusing to let the energy explode out. Amazingly, his layers of control contained it. But he couldn't hold on forever.

Containment was only step one. Now, starting at Kelvin's extremities, the very ends of the energy's path, Jim squeezed harder. Then he moved farther up the power lines and squeezed again. Bit by bit, he took the energy that was trying to explode out and forced it to feed back into the source—the Chaos Merchant's battery.

It was like trying to catch an explosion and squeeze it into a tube of toothpaste. With every step, the energy battled against him, fighting to burst forth and be free, to destroy all in its path. Jim couldn't hear. He couldn't see. He couldn't recall anything beyond this moment. Were seconds going by, or hours?

Finally, the last waves of power snapped back into place. Fully charged again, the battery fought harder than ever to fulfill its purpose.

Jim was about to black out. If he didn't do this now, it was over.

With a cry of exertion, he wrapped every shred of his will around the battery, yanked it out of Kelvin's chest, and flung it through the door of the utility closet.

"Natalie!" he shouted.

Still blind, he could only hear the rumble and hope that Natalie's shield had dropped into place over the closet door.

There was an instant of silence.

Then a wave of force hit him like a thunderclap.

TWENTY THREE

EVERYTHING hurt. Jim's eyes felt pasted shut, like he'd spent the last decade in a coma. Groaning, he cracked them open with effort.

Through dazed, bleary eyes, he observed what used to be a server room. Now it was half server room, half rubble. Natalie's rock shield must have absorbed most of the blast, because there seemed to be gravel everywhere.

Jim lay on his back amid the wreckage. He tried to brace his hands on the floor and lean up, and discovered his wrists were bound by a zip tie.

"Uh," he said eloquently, blinking hard.

His eyes slowly came into better focus, revealing Kelvin laid out on the floor nearby, pale and unmoving. Was he dead? Jim lurched up to his knees.

"Kelvin? Wake up, man."

"He can't," Zoe said.

Jim turned toward the voice and almost toppled, awash in dizziness. Zoe, Natalie, and Eli sat on the floor and leaned heavily against the wall, each wearing bandages–probably cuts from flying shrapnel. The team had survived, at least.

The team that he'd let down, maybe fatally. He could see it in their downcast eyes, their sagging posture. They were trapped and losing hope. Zoe would barely look at him when she spoke.

"Kelvin's wound was small, fortunately," she said. "I patched it with trauma foam and sedated him. We'll hide him behind some wreckage when we break out of here. Ironically, he may survive longer than we do."

"How long was I out?" Jim asked.

"Only a few minutes," Eli said. "Just long enough to get everyone patched up, including you."

"Me?" Now that he was aware, Jim felt something against his right temple. He reached up with bound hands and found two butterfly stitches stuck to his head. "Oh."

"You took a nasty hit," Natalie said. "We were worried."

"Not that you didn't deserve it," Zoe muttered.

Well, that explained the dizziness and disorientation. Jim held his hands toward Zoe.

"I assume this is your work, too. Is there anything you don't hide in that suit?" He attempted a halfhearted grin. "What about snacks?"

He got three flat looks in response. The message was clear—he'd lost the right to crack jokes when he lied, and when people were about to die. He glanced at the display and found it, too, had shattered.

"Nine minutes," Eli said. "I'm still keeping track."

Feeling twice as heavy now, Jim melted back down like a puddle. Eyes downcast, he studied his bound hands and started talking.

"My name is James Riven, but as a kid, I was known by another name. Summer—my older sister—was Lock, and I was Lode." No one told him to shut up, so he kept going. Might as well confess everything. They deserved that much. "We just wanted to help Highreach. Use our little powers for something good, something real. It's still crazy to me, but we actually started making a difference. We weren't ready for powered villains, but we chased gangs out of town, shut down crime rings, that kind of stuff. It felt good doing that together, and over time, we made a little name for ourselves. And then Skypuncher showed up at our door."

That got their attention. No one had been looking at him, but now he heard them shift, felt their eyes on him.

"He personally invited Summer to compete in the first Dare. She made being a hero look easy, and before we knew it, she wasn't our hometown hero anymore. She was part of a Prism, working for the Spectrum. Our parents were so proud. I was, too, but . . . well, mostly I just missed my sister. I tried going out solo as Lode, but without Summer, it was never the same. I kept thinking . . . maybe I'd get recruited, too, and we could work together again."

He swallowed, preparing himself. The story only got worse from here.

"Then Framework attacked Sydney, and my sister's Prism responded."

"Whoa." Natalie leaned back, eyes wide. "I was only a kid, but even I remember that. How many heroes died in that battle?"

"Too many," Eli said. "That was a bad day."

"Framework killed Anchor," Zoe said quietly. "Before that, I thought no one could kill one of the Spectrum."

"Nine thousand people in Sydney died," Jim said. "In all the chaos, it took them days to figure out how many heroes had fallen. My parents wouldn't turn off the news, waiting for word. Any word. Then, for the second time, Skypuncher knocked on our door."

"Oh, no." Natalie put her hands over her mouth.

Jim nodded. The backs of his eyes were stinging now. He tried to bottle up the remembered emotions and failed utterly.

"After that, it was like a bomb slowly exploding in our lives. My mom collapsed in on herself until one day she walked out the door and never came back. My dad drank himself to death. I tried to be Lode again, but just . . . couldn't. The last time, I watched a crew break into a diamond dealer, and did nothing. Didn't even want to. That thing inside me–the hero thing I used to have–it was just gone. So I turned around and went home, cut the costume to pieces and burned it. I was done with heroes. That was someone else's life."

"But you bought Versus," Eli said. "A hero bar."

"It used to be a hero bar," Jim corrected. "Now it's a joke, and I've let it stay that way on purpose. My dad left me enough money to invest in something. When I heard the bar was on the market, I knew it was a perfect fit. What better reminder of how little a hero's legacy matters than some broken-down old place where has-beens slap each other in front of drunks? So, now I serve booze and mediocre food, and no one asks me to die for a world that'll forget my name the next week."

"But you're here now," Zoe said, her tone implying how little sense that made.

"I'm not trying out, if that's what you mean. I came because Lord Neon told me there was more to the story about Summer. That she was still out there somewhere, and I could only find the truth here. So he gave me a fake identity and an invitation."

"Why would he do that?" Zoe said. "Why not just tell you the truth?"

"Who knows why he does anything? The guy's a sphinx. But his reasons didn't matter if there was even a chance it was true. I had to find out. I *had* to. And because of that, I . . . chose finding the truth over everything else." Jim sagged, emptied out like a balloon. All his secrets had spilled out now. "I told you I'm not a hero. Guess I proved it."

"Do you really turn things on and off?" Natalie asked. "I mean, what you did to Kelvin, I still don't understand it."

Okay, so maybe not *all* his secrets.

"I'm a type of Electric Controller. If it runs on electricity, I can tell it to do things. Within my limits, of course. Though, um, that brings up something else that no one knows." He took a deep breath. This part scared him, but he'd lost the right to keep secrets from them. "I'm also a Vessel."

Zoe's eyebrows climbed. "Oh."

Natalie frowned. "What's that mean?"

"Vessels are an extremely rare kind of parahuman," Eli explained. "Your capacity always stays right around 7.8, right?"

"Right," Natalie said.

"Well, a Vessel has a base power level, but it's only their *resting* capacity. They can increase their power when certain conditions are met. Correct, Jim?"

Jim nodded. "My resting capacity is 3.6. But the more electricity I absorb, the higher it goes. I don't actually know my upper limit. Quit the life before it was fully tested."

Natalie frowned as if that was the saddest thing she'd ever heard. "You don't even know your own power, and you spend life hiding behind a bar?"

Jim looked down, surprised that he felt embarrassed. "Well . . ."

Crawling across the floor, Natalie sat by Jim and wrapped her arms around him, head on his shoulder.

"I'm sorry, Jim. About Summer. About everything." She sniffled. "We never really know someone's pain by looking at them, do we?"

"Too true," Eli said heavily.

"Thanks, Nat," Jim said, nudging her. "I think you're the happiest person I know."

Natalie moved to respond but stopped short, as if inside she was wrestling with something. Her mouth opened and closed and opened again.

"I . . . I got kicked out at fourteen," she said. "My family rejected me."

"Well," Jim said. "Now I feel like a jerk."

"It's okay." Natalie squeezed his arm. "In the end, it was for the best. They . . . I mean, my family is . . ."

"The Seven Serpents," Eli said. "That's your family?"

"How did you know that?"

"Natalie Yu. Your last name. I'm around heroes enough to hear things."

"What are the Seven Serpents?" Jim said.

"Organized crime," Zoe said. "They're big in Cloudreach, with ties back to Hong Kong and mainland China. I, uh, may have retrieved a few items for them in my old life. And *from* them."

"That's them," Natalie said. "When my powers manifested, they couldn't bring me into the business fast enough. I hated it so much, but I was a kid. How could I go against my own family? But when I was fourteen, they forced me to help them rob a bank and . . . and one of their enforcers hurt someone."

Sniffling again, she wiped away a tear.

"That was it. I couldn't stand it anymore. So I gave the police evidence that helped them arrest the whole crew. When I got immunity, it was pretty obvious who turned them in. My mother almost killed me, but my father stopped her, and instead they banished me. I've been on my own ever since."

Jim blew out a breath. "Alone since you were fourteen. Wow."

"Yeah." Sitting up straighter, Natalie put on a brighter face. "But I get to be a hero. If I have to live in my car, that's okay. At least I'm helping. That's all I want to do. That's why I'm here."

Jim decided then that Natalie Yu might not be the happiest person he'd ever met, but she might just be the *best*. Suddenly, his own choices felt petty, selfish. He put his arm around her and squeezed the way he used to with Summer.

"If it helps," he said. "You're definitely *my* hero."

"Aw, thanks." Making a fist, Natalie softly bumped it against his chin. "You're all right yourself, kid."

They chuckled together, and the room felt a little brighter.

"I got someone killed," Zoe blurted, then recoiled. "Um, I mean, I didn't kill them—I don't do that—but it was my fault."

She stared at them defensively, as if expecting condemnation or some kind of fight. When neither came, she relaxed enough to keep talking.

"I was always a talented thief, ever since I was a kid. In and out like a shadow, no mess, no drama. That's why people hired me. Things got stickier if a rival thief came after the same item, but I could usually handle that. Until . . ."

She paused, and her chest heaved with emotion.

"Randall Snow–this new guy who wanted to make a name for himself. About a year ago, he crashed one of my jobs, and he wouldn't back off. I tried to shut the whole thing down, but he kept coming at me and I defended myself and . . . well. I won't bore you with the details. I'm here and he's not. After that, I kind of started to unravel. Tried to keep going like everything was fine, but I was self-destructing. One night in Highreach, I botched a job *bad* and ended up coming face-to-face with Lawspeaker."

The group blew out a collective breath.

"Wow," Jim said. "You got pinched by the Judge? What was she like?"

"As relentless and terrifying as everyone says," Zoe said. "More, actually. I didn't stand a chance."

Lawspeaker, a heroine in a faceless white mask and vivid red armor, was Highreach's most ardent and infamous protector. She was also as scary and ferocious as a hero could be while still being called a hero. Though no one had ever figured out the specifics of her powers, few met her and came away victorious.

"And yet," Zoe continued. "When she had me down–when she could've crushed me–she didn't. She talked to me. I broke and told her everything, and we sat on that rooftop until sunrise. When she could've tossed me in jail, instead she spent all night helping me see that I could rebuild myself into something better. A year later, when she thought I was ready, she sponsored my invitation to the Dare."

Zoe scrubbed at her cheek.

"I still struggle with it. Sometimes I see Randall Snow's face when I close my eyes. And sometimes I see things and *really* want to steal them. But I'm getting better. I *want* to be better. That's why I'm here."

A look of understanding passed between them. Understanding and forgiveness and brotherhood. Sisterhood? Familyhood? Was personhood a word? Either way, Jim thought they might be able to be a real team after all, if they could pull themselves together and figure a way out of this room without getting ambushed.

One of them, though, had stayed quiet during their surprise therapy session. All eyes turned to Eli.

Leaning away, he held up his hands. "Don't look at me. I just work here." He seemed to look inward, turning thoughtful, and then he stood. "But I'll die before I let myself sit while people get hurt. Especially those kids in the atrium who came here to serve the world."

Natalie bounded to her feet. "I'm with you, Eli!"

Zoe shrugged and stood up. "I'm not a thief anymore. I'm a freakin' hero. And heroes save people."

Now they all looked at Jim, expectant, and he felt a flash of sympathy for Eli when they'd done the same thing to him. Did Jim really want this?

Does it matter? Stand up, idiot.

Climbing to his feet, he held his hands out to Zoe, who sliced through his bonds with practiced ease. He gave a sort of half-salute.

"Heroic speech," he said with an air of drama. "Inspiring words. Personal breakthroughs and all that good guy stuff. Assurance of victory, et cetera."

Zoe rolled her eyes, but this time she didn't hide her smile. "How long do we have?"

"Four minutes," Eli said.

"Okay, guys," Jim said. "I don't know how, but let's bust out of this room, save some lives, and give evil a wedgie it'll never forget."

"Um." Sheepishly, Natalie raised her hand. "About getting out of here—I have an idea."

TWENTY FOUR

"GATHER in, everyone," Natalie said. "Squeeze closer."

"Two minutes to go," Eli said, sounding nervous. "This is insane."

"Oh, good," Jim said. "Then it matches everything else today."

"Don't make it too small," Zoe said. "Or we won't be able to fit the others."

"No worries," Natalie said. "I'll make it bigger when we get there. But for speed and penetrating power, there's a particular shape we need." She looked at Eli. "You're sure it's right above us?"

"More or less. Should be close enough, given our limited time to plan."

"Plan? Ha! Good one," Jim said.

In the center of their makeshift hero cluster, Natalie raised her hands. "Ready, everyone?"

"No," Eli said. "But do it anyway."

"Okay. Stay still."

Closing her eyes, Natalie went taut. Deep breath in . . . slow breath out . . .

"One minute to go, Natalie," Eli urged.

Natalie stretched her arms wide, palms out. Another slow breath.

"Natalie–" Eli began.

"Yah!" she cried.

Sounds like crackling ice and a rushing river filled the room. On the floor, a translucent crystalline structure grew in a circle around them. Natalie's palms turned upward and the structure grew, forming what began as a sphere and resolved into a teardrop as it closed over their heads.

The team now stood inside a hollow teardrop made of diamond, with the top coming to a wicked lance-like point.

Natalie looked to Zoe. "Ready?"

Zoe pressed her palms against the jewel. "Just say when."

Tensing, Natalie grunted, and the teardrop lurched upward. "Now!"

Inky blackness spread from Zoe's hands. Aethyr coated the pod, and their movement went from a lurch to a launch. They shot up like a cannonball to smash through the ceiling, trailing steam from the heat of using Aethyr.

The blackness receded, revealing that they had left the server room behind and were now lodged in the superstructure between levels.

Eyes closed in concentration, Eli pressed fingers to his temple. "Another dozen feet. Hit it hard and we'll punch through."

"Two more rounds?" Zoe said.

"No time. We've gotta get there now." Gritting her teeth, Natalie strained. The teardrop lurched up twice as hard as before.

Zoe followed her lead. Blackness surrounded them, hotter this time, and they flew up like a rocket.

The teardrop hit something with bone-shaking force and sliced through. Clashing sounds of rock and metal assaulted the team from all sides. Then there was a final impact, and they ground to a stop.

Zoe's Aethyr receded to reveal that they had punched up through the Lighthouse, and reached the Torch. Now several sets of eyes stared up at them in shock.

It seemed their ascent hadn't stopped when they broke through the atrium floor. They had kept going until the point of the teardrop had pierced Skypuncher's statue right through his outstretched hand. Bad news–they now hovered a dozen feet above the floor. Good news–they were only a small leap away from the stage where Geometron's captives were about to be executed.

Jim surveyed the scene, awash in adrenaline as he estimated their chances of survival.

No time for that. Just move. Let's go be heroes.

Say that again, brain, and I'll force you to watch Downton Abbey. The entire series.

Geometron was the first to recover from their entrance. Her shocked expression became a snarl, red eye flaring.

"Thirty seconds," Eli said.

Natalie touched the side of the teardrop. The surface flowed open like water and then solidified again, like ice freezing over. With battle cries, Jim and company dove out of the teardrop and leapt into action.

They all knew their parts. Natalie would stay in the teardrop and expand it enough to fit everyone, preparing for a quick and probably desperate escape. Zoe would engage Geometron and buy them time. Which put Jim and Eli on hostage rescue.

Jim had to focus on his part and trust his teammates to do theirs. The three young Dare contestants trembled, strapped to stone pillars with multiple restraints and wrapped with layer upon layer of exposed power cables. The cables collected into an arm-thick bundle near Kalliope, which then connected to a power relay on the nearest wall. Jim felt the energy crackling inside the relay, waiting to be unleashed. When the countdown ended, those cables would deliver a staggering surge of power.

"Jim," Eli said from behind one pillar, where he examined the restraints. He started undoing them, but there was a heavy look in his eyes. "These bonds are complex. There's . . . not enough time to free them all."

"What?! No!" the young hero beside Kalliope wailed. "Please, I don't want to die here!"

Ten seconds left. Desperately, Jim probed the power relay and studied the bundle of cables more closely, searching for any weakness he could exploit. The system had too many redundancies and backups to shut them all down in so little time, and the power surge would be large enough to kill anyone who touched those cables.

. . . or almost anyone. Maybe.

Have you ever handled that much power before?

Does it matter?

Jim guessed not. With a wistful shrug, he stepped past Kalliope and wrapped both arms tightly around the bundle of cables. A death hug.

Seven seconds.

"No, please," Kalliope said to Jim. "Go. Someone has to survive this."

Three seconds.

Heroes really do suck.

Two seconds.

Especially Skypuncher.

One second.

What a jackass.

Fire filled Jim's veins. His vision flashed white. Somebody screamed. Definitely not him, but somebody. And even if it was him . . . shut up.

His teeth chattered. His muscles felt like they were tearing apart fiber by fiber. Electricity roared through him like a raging river, threatening to scour him away.

He squeezed the cables tighter, working bit by bit to wrap his ability around the power and contain it. It fought back like a wild animal yearning to burst free. Jim's entire being stretched until it was paper thin, spanning the length and breadth of the Lighthouse.

Then, when he had stretched nearly to breaking, everything snapped back into place. Suddenly Jim was Jim again, his mind and power back inside his body, still wrapped around the live wires.

Except now there was more of Jim than before. Everything about him had multiplied. Speed of thought. Range and depth of senses. Power and control. It felt as if the Lighthouse were in his grip now, and if he wanted to, he could simply reach out and flip the switch.

He opened his eyes. Eli and the young heroes gaped as if Jim had suddenly grown ten feet tall. Peering down at himself, he understood why. From the power relay all the way to his grip, the unshielded cables crackled and glowed with surging blue-white energy. Where before that energy would have fried the Dare contestants, now it twisted and writhed across his skin, coating his body.

He chuckled. When he spoke, his voice vibrated with power. "Hey, this kinda tickles."

"Villain scum!" Geometron bellowed.

There was a red flash. Jim turned to see Zoe smack against a wall and crumple. Then Geometron whipped around to face Jim.

"Well," Jim said. "Crap."

The Spectrum hero pointed his way. Her thrusters fired, depositing her on the stage mere steps away. Holding Jim's gaze, she raised her left arm and a razor-sharp blade extended from her wrist.

"Fine," she said. "I'll do it the old-fashioned way."

She drew her arm back, preparing to strike at Kalliope's heart. The young hero kept a brave face. Even as her lip trembled, as a tear slid down her cheek, she stared Geometron in the eye and did not beg. She only waited for the end, standing as tall as she could.

Geometron struck.

Jim's thoughts raced at the speed of light. He was a kid again, standing at the mirror and admiring his costume for the first time. Summer was by his side, everything about her shiny and bright. Her eyes, so young and full of hope, like Kalliope's probably were before everything went to hell. They were going to save the world, or at least their little corner of it.

He blinked and years passed. He could only watch, helpless, as the battle razed half of downtown Sydney to the ground. So many bright, young, heroic faces would know agony before the end. Before they never came home. Before their families had to wonder for the rest of their lives what really happened that day.

His thoughts raced ahead to the future, to the days and months and years after the catastrophe that had struck the Lighthouse today. To Kalliope's family, who would eventually hear a cleaned-up version of what really happened on the news. They would clutch each other, terrified, hoping their little girl would appear and tell them everything was fine. There would be a knock on their front door, but it wouldn't be her. It would never be her again.

No, Jim's brain said over and over again, *no no no NO **NO***, until it became a howl that had to burst from him. Like a beast, he shouted with every cell in his body.

His attention focused down, ignoring every cable and relay and motor and light bulb and power source in the Lighthouse, and shining like a spotlight on Geometron–on the part of her that was machine beyond most human understanding. A machine that no one had ever hacked or deciphered or broken down.

With enormous power surging through him, with a young hero's life in his hands, Jim pushed his senses harder than he'd ever thought possible. He peeled his right hand from the bundle of cables and reached toward Geometron.

Suddenly, he saw the complex shielding around her machinery, perceiving with his mind's eye how they overlapped like electromagnetic armor. He battered at that shield's weak points from all sides until it gave way, and in less than a blink, he knew every inch of her machinery as if he'd built it himself. He saw the real Geometron underneath, how she worked, who and what she really was.

Huh. Interesting.

His outstretched hand clenched into a fist. Geometron froze, her blade half an inch from Kalliope's chest. She grunted, lurching unnaturally, trying to force her blade forward and failing.

Wait, he'd done it? Jim barely believed it himself. He'd actually stopped Geometron! He laughed in disbelief.

"No. It's not possible," Geometron growled. "Fight me for real, you coward!"

"Uh, no thank you," Jim said. "I'm fine right here."

"You idiot," she spat. "You think you've seen my full power? Soon I will be free, and then you will die."

"I can't believe I used to have a crush on you," Jim said. "I mean, I still do, kind of. But I'm going to seriously rethink that if you murder me."

The hero's eyes flicked over Jim's shoulder. A sly grin crept across her face. "Or maybe I won't have to kill you myself."

Jim heard footsteps approach from behind. Focusing so completely on his foe, he'd failed to keep an eye on his surroundings. Now, with one arm wrapped around the cables and the other stretched toward Geometron, he couldn't move or he'd lose control of both. He forced himself to keep calm.

Royal Justice and his punchable face stepped into view. "You dare threaten the Mistress of Machines?"

Jim worked to bury his fear. "Ah, Captain Eggplant. What took you so long?"

"Oh, I love a good old-fashioned execution." Drawing twin swords, he faced Jim and offered a fencing salute. "Consider yourself honored, Interruptor. These blades have drawn far better blood than yours. Blood that–*oof!*"

From off stage, a cord flew into view and wrapped around Royal Justice. Cinching tight around his torso, it dragged him to the floor. Zoe came into view, wearing her full Moxie suit, mask and all, and reeled the ridiculous hero in like a prized fish. She threw Jim a quick salute, and he nodded back. Now he could focus on Geometron.

Which was good, because their fight had only just begun.

TWENTY FIVE

ROYAL Justice sliced through the cord with ease and swung to chop Zoe in half. She danced back, and with a flick of her wrists ejected two kevlar-weaved carbon fiber daggers. She gripped them in time to parry her foe's next attack.

"What, no opening salute?" Zoe said. "I thought you fancied yourself a man of honor."

"Honor is wasted on the honor-less, villain. You will receive no quarter here."

The two of them became a flurry of fists and feet and blades darting in and out, searching for weak points and holes in each other's defenses. With blinding speed and ferocity, they traded blows while dancing between the other's sharp edges. Zoe took a fist to the chin and delivered a jab to his solar plexus. He elbowed her sternum and she struck a bundle of nerves near his kidney.

He was good. Zoe had to admit that. Fast and brutal enough that they stalemated, neither gaining significant ground. But she was patient. Her moment would come. She was smaller and younger–eventually, he would underestimate her and overplay his hand. Then they would see–

The hero's left blade sliced in for the kill, close enough to touch the collar of her trench coat. Despite the nanomesh armor weave, his blade cut right through it. Zoe felt a flash of fear. This was getting real now.

Before Royal Justice could turn the blade and slice her throat, Zoe kneed him in the gut. He grunted, hunching over his middle, while she dropped into a back handspring. As her body spun, she loosed a wave of shock darts in his direction. He recovered quickly enough to bat them from the air—all except one, which latched onto his chest plate. He jolted and shuddered before knocking it loose.

Zoe slid in close and jabbed at her opponent's hands, looking to disarm him. Royal Justice countered with a wicked head-butt, knocking Zoe back a step, which gave him room to bring his blades to bear and clang them together. Energy burst from the weapons to hit her square-on.

Zoe fell back again, rattling her head to clear away the purple flashes and blurred vision. She regained control just in time to see Royal Justice swing at her neck.

She dropped and turned her dodge into a spin, sweeping at his legs. He leapt high and laughed in derision, easily evading while striking downward with his swords. Except Zoe wasn't there anymore. As he leapt, she rolled beneath his feet and came up behind him. The moment his feet touched the floor, she intertwined her arms and daggers with his arms and swords, effectively locking his arms behind his back with his blades pointed away from her.

"Yield and this ends," she said.

"This only ends with you dead."

He flicked both wrists and his blades *reversed*, sliding through the hilts until they burst through the pommel. With a shocked cry, Zoe twisted away from the steel. She avoided the blade aimed at her chest, but took a cut above her eye from the other. An inch different, a microsecond slower, and it would have been over.

Too surprised, Zoe released him and dropped back a step. Royal Justice whirled with a shout and swung hard. His swords cleaved through both of her daggers.

He drove forward, striking for all her vital organs while Zoe backpedaled and twisted between the storm of metal. Another back handspring to buy the moment she needed, and then a titanium baton was in her hands. Instead of retreating, now she batted away his attacks.

Stalemated again. And again, Zoe had to admit that he was good. She could see in her opponent's eyes that he was realizing the same about her. Except, while she felt begrudgingly impressed that such a blowhard could actually deliver on his threats, Royal Justice only grew more outraged that she wasn't dead yet.

Her back thumped against a wall. Nowhere left to go. Bellowing in rage, Royal Justice swung full-force and chopped her baton in half. He placed the tip of one blade over her heart and the other under her chin.

Regaining his superior air, he chuckled. "You were always going to lose. This is an honest battle, nothing to steal. And my family's blades have never met a villain they could not cut."

Leaving the one blade pressed to her chest, he drew back the other and struck.

Geometron growled. "I'm going to break you in half."

"You're really pretty," Jim said, straining.

"Die!"

Though not touching, they stood locked together, will against will, power against power. Teeth gritted, pushing back with all her might, Geometron battled to move while Jim battled to hold her in place.

"Halfway there, Jim!" Eli called. "Hold on."

He had freed the young hero farthest from Jim. She was scrambling into the teardrop, which Natalie had enlarged. Now Eli worked on the second captive.

Jim had never absorbed even close to this much electricity before, and certainly not for this long, and absolutely not while using it to battle one of the most celebrated heroes on the planet. His body had become a conduit for raw power, his consciousness hanging on by a fingernail, to be scoured away if he lost focus for an instant. All while Geometron pitted her strength and experience against his. He could feel her fighting him, constantly reconfiguring herself to escape his grip.

A chess match at the speed of thought. If he fell behind, she would overcome him.

"What is it they call you? Interruptor?" the hero taunted, as if the name left a sour taste in her mouth. "A forgettable moniker for a man who'll be forgotten."

"You're right, it's much better to be named after a high school math class. Maybe I'll change mine to Introduction to Spanish. What do you think?"

Geometron seethed. "I think you're about to die."

"No! *Por qué*?!"

Screaming, Geometron regathered herself and threw all her might against him. It felt like he'd been sucker punched in the gut. He nearly lost his grip.

She was winning. Her power was overwhelming. Slowly but inevitably, the tide would turn in her favor.

There was no way around it. He had to do something crazy. And there was really only one thing crazier than what he was already doing.

He couldn't help chuckling. "You know, the world may forget me. Actually, I hope they do. But I know one thing for sure—you'll never forget *this*."

Casting his senses toward the power relay that was feeding him, Jim commanded all its fail-safes and limiters to shut down, then threw the virtual gates wide open. A high-pitched whine radiated from the relay as an unbridled wave of electricity roared through it. The power lines glowed brighter as the wave hit Jim. He worked to push through the nausea, using every shred of will to open his ability wider and process more power. Groaning, he clung to Geometron with the desperation of a man who simply could not fail.

Her machinery audibly groaned as she fought against him. For the first time, her rage also showed a tinge of uncertainty.

"How are you doing this?" she asked.

"You first." Jim nodded to her physique. "How'd you get that way? Were you bitten by a radioactive Best Buy?"

"Holding all that power, and you can still crack jokes. You're not some hero wannabe. Who are you really?"

"My name is Lode. You knew my sister."

Geometron's eyes widened.

Despite his agony, Jim managed a defiant grin. "And this is *my* house. You just rent a room."

Zoe's insides bathed in heat, a familiar scorching sensation. As she opened that door in her mind and Aethyr flowed through to embrace her, the blade of Royal Justice seemed to cut toward her neck in slow motion.

She'd only been using her Striker and Dodger powers before, leaving out the Aethyr augment. It was the only way to truly learn how her enemy fought. Now, though, she had his measure.

And it was her time.

As blackness closed around her, turning her vision red, Zoe reached into her trench coat and gripped the hilt of a hidden weapon. Her Aethyr somehow communed with the Aethyr layered into the dual-edged blade, connecting her to it in a way she'd never felt before. The sensation was . . . too incredible to think about right now. She put it aside for later, and instead became a blur of motion.

In a blink, Zoe parried and stepped aside so that her opponent's blade bit into the wall where she'd been standing. Royal Justice fell back a half-step, momentarily confused. Then his eyes found Zoe, and as she released her Aethyr, he spotted the weapon in her hand.

His face contorted with rage. "You dare to wield Dark Sympathy?!"

Zoe shrugged. She'd turned over a new leaf, but in this case she hadn't been able to help herself. "Well, once a thief . . ."

Then she moved. Absorbing microbursts of Aethyr, she flowed around Royal Justice like a storm wind, alternating randomly between normal and Aethyr-augmented movement. Dark Sympathy carved through the air like an extension of her arm, darting in and out, slipping past her foe's defenses to deliver dozens of small nicks and cuts.

First she took his left sword, and shortly after, his right. As they clanged to the floor and their purple glow winked out, Zoe danced behind Royal Justice and swung Dark Sympathy . . . reversing her grip for a pommel strike to his neck. With a grunt, the hero fell to his knees.

Zoe whirled to a stop in front of him, tip of the sword pressed to his chest. Though he stared up at her with hatred, she could see the fear behind his eyes.

She released the last of her Aethyr, and the burning sensation faded with it. She was actually a little out of breath.

"I'm impressed," she conceded. "Not many people make me work for it."

Royal Justice spat on her boot. "Do what comes naturally to your kind. Finish it."

Zoe leaned closer. "Remember this moment. Because if I *were* a villain, you'd no longer have a head."

With a flourish, she sheathed Dark Sympathy and turned her back on Royal Justice. Then she reconsidered and spun.

"Though, I never said I was a paragon of virtue, either."

She kicked out like a snapping whip, and the toe of her boot cracked against his temple. He collapsed, unconscious.

"Sweet dreams, douchebag."

Zoe gave herself a single moment to savor the victory. She suspected there might be repercussions for humiliating a Prism hero, but in this moment, it was hard to care. He had it coming.

As her battle focus receded, her senses widened to take in the rest of the atrium. During her fight, she hadn't been able to spare a thought for what else may be happening. Now, though, she looked to the stage and her jaw dropped.

Jim glowed like a coruscating blue-white star, one hand stretched toward Geometron while he clung to the bundle of power cables. The Spectrum hero vibrated with superhuman effort, but wasn't moving an inch.

It seemed there was more that Jim Riven hadn't shared about himself.

That would have to wait. They had a fight to finish.

"Soon, you'll be mine," Geometron promised. "I know you feel it."

"This is the weirdest date ever," Jim replied.

He did feel it. She was clawing back control bit by bit. It was only a matter of time before she overcame him. But he couldn't let it show or she'd only press harder.

"And you," Geometron cast her flaring red eye on Kalliope. "Pretty young thing. You will die screaming."

Trembling, Kalliope swallowed hard. "I used to look up to you."

A tear rolled down her cheek. But as she spoke, Jim caught movement from the corner of his eye. Kalliope's body was bound to the pillar, wrapped nearly head to toe. Nearly–but not completely. While her arms were cinched up to the wrist, her hands were still free enough to turn her palm upward, fingers curled as if to grip something spherical. In that space between her fingers, the air began to warp.

Restraints clattered to the stage. The second Dare contestant burst free, arms up as if to strike at Geometron. Reaching around the pillar, Eli yanked the boy by the collar and spun him toward the teardrop.

"That's a good way to die, son. Now, into the pod!" As the boy reluctantly complied, Eli rushed to Kalliope's pillar and got to work. "Hang on, Jim. Only one to go."

"He won't last that long," Geometron taunted, casting her malevolent grin at Jim. "Will you, sweetie?"

Jim reached for a witty comeback and found he'd run out. All he could do was hold on.

"Even if some of you escape, you'll never beat the Dare," Geometron said. "Every path to your goal is a deathtrap. There's only one sure way to get there, and you'll never find it. It's hidden like buried treasure."

Jim fell to his knees, nearly spent.

"Yes, it won't be long," Geometron purred. "Rest now. Give in . . . like your sister did."

Jim's head whipped toward her, eyes wide. And in his instant of distraction, Geometron gained more ground. She lifted her chin in smug satisfaction.

"Oh yes, I did know her. I was there that day in Sydney, and I saw the moment she–"

"Jim, drop!" Zoe called.

Everything seemed to happen at once. Jim fell back as a dark shape flew overhead. Zoe landed next to the power cables and chopped through the bundle in one hard swing. The energy surging through him winked out.

His concentration slipped and then shattered as Geometron pressed her advantage. She lurched, suddenly free, and for a split second she wavered between striking at Jim or her original target.

Kalliope's fingers uncurled. An earsplitting sound filled the air, like the amplified strum of an electric guitar, and a shock-wave leapt from her palm to strike Geometron right between the eyes. The hero's head snapped back. She staggered backward with a gasp and toppled off the stage.

There she lay, dazed and moaning.

TWENTY SIX

"YOU literally hugged a death trap." Zoe stared down at Jim. "Even for you, that was pretty dumb."

Lying on his back, Jim blinked hard. His vision had gone all wonky, like he was seeing the world through a funhouse mirror. And when he looked up at Zoe, there was a weird glow coming from inside her chest.

A little green ball of light.

He rattled his head, smacking his temple with the heel of his palm. The waviness receded and the light disappeared.

"Hey, how am I supposed to know something's dangerous unless I hug it?" He tapped his chin in thought. "Maybe that's why I keep getting bitten by stray dogs and cats and hobos."

Tapping his chin brought his wrist into view. Jim's Gauge was no longer there. A quick glance around the stage revealed that it had fallen off, but not before being melted by the immense surge of electricity.

"Well," he said. "I hope this isn't a you-break-it-you-buy-it situation."

Zoe tapped a button and her mask folded away. Her voice softened. "That was a brave thing you did. Some might even say heroic."

From his prone position, Jim reached out and poked her ankle. "You take that back. If I could move, those would be fighting words."

"I'm more dangerous than I look."

"Well, how would I know when we haven't hugged?"

Shaking her head, Zoe helped him to his feet. "Maybe we'll get to that later."

"Was that flirting? Be careful with me. I've been hurt before." Jim pointed at Geometron, who lay still. "Literally. By her, just now."

"There," Eli said. "Finally."

Kalliope's bonds dropped away. She leapt into Jim's arms, hugging tightly enough to hurt and peppering him with a million thank-you's. Zoe took a step back, looking amused as Jim endured the Death Squeeze of Gratitude.

He gave a helpless shrug. "Well, at least I know she's not dangerous."

Zoe laughed, then covered her mouth and looked away to hide it.

"Sorry I couldn't go any faster," Eli said. "Never seen restraints like that."

"Don't worry about it," Jim said.

"Yeah, no one's prepared for any of this," Zoe said.

Letting go at last, Kalliope stepped back and cast a desperate look at her rescuers. "What's happening? Did the Spectrum really turn bad?"

Before they could reply, a shrill whistle rang out from the teardrop.

"Yo," Natalie called, leaning through the opening. "Anyone feel like escaping with their lives while they can?"

Jim didn't hear the replies. While Natalie spoke, something in the room changed. His Controller senses were exhausted and seared and nowhere even approaching accurate right now, but still it was there . . . possibly in *that* direction . . .

Turning, he struggled to focus. It felt like trying to lift weights after he'd already bench pressed a car. He squinted, aiming his thoughts until it hurt.

There. That was it. Geometron wasn't moving, but she was awake, and she'd doomed them all over again.

"Oh, crap," Jim said. "We've got to move. She just–"

Turbula, Astro-Ninja, Heatsink, and a fourth Prism hero that Jim didn't recognize rushed in from four directions to surround them. The fifth point of their evil little star completed when Geometron stood up to join them, looking far too satisfied.

"Just sent a distress call," Jim finished, crestfallen.

"Now, now, don't pout," Geometron said. "This won't be any fun unless you fight back."

"Please, Azita," Eli said. "If you have any humanity left . . ."

"Ready," Geometron snapped, raising her arm.

Her minions prepared to strike. Giving a weary sigh, Jim stood back to back with his teammates and Kalliope and prepared to do what he could until it was over.

Kalliope aimed a molten glare at Geometron. "I knocked you out once. I'll do it again."

Laughing with violent glee, Geometron dropped her arm.

From somewhere behind Jim, a sizzling yellow beam arced across the atrium and slammed full-force into Turbula. She didn't even have time to scream before it smashed her through the wall.

"What?!" Geometron cried.

Someone loosed a battle cry, followed by heavy footsteps and whooshing winds and a dozen other sounds of power. They poured in from every doorway, arrayed in every color imaginable, each shouting their own taunts and cries for justice. Jim barely had time to process what was happening before the corrupted heroes that had surrounded them suddenly found themselves surrounded.

Nearly a dozen Dare contestants. Somehow, they must have found each other and banded together to mount a rescue. Now they descended on the Prism heroes, and the atrium exploded into a war zone of exotic powers.

Jim still knew he wasn't a hero. He still didn't want any part of this life. But standing in the eye of the storm, beholding the spectacle around him, even he had a hard time not being moved. Surely these were heroes at their best.

A man in golden armor hovered into view, floating through the din with balls of yellow energy spinning above his outstretched palms. His eyes burned with what Jim could only describe as righteous anger. Placing himself between Jim and Geometron, he pointed at the hero.

"You issued a challenge," his voice boomed, his very presence radiating raw power. "I, Recompense, have come to answer it."

Staring up at him, even Geometron seemed hesitant. Recompense moved toward her, then stopped and glanced over his shoulder at Jim.

"Weren't you escaping with her captives?" he asked.

Jim didn't have to be told twice.

"Fall back to the pod," he said.

Quickly as they could, Eli, Zoe, Kalliope, and Jim fled to their escape. As Jim climbed inside the crystalline teardrop, before Natalie closed the opening, he turned to look back at their rescuer.

Recompense squared off with his quarry and beckoned, inviting her to make the first move. Burying her obvious trepidation, Geometron braced herself, shouted in rage and leapt.

The teardrop closed. Its walls turned to black and radiated heat.

"Hang on!" Natalie cried.

Then they dropped.

Kelvin gasped. His eyes flew open, full of panic.

"Welcome back," Zoe said, pulling the dart from his chest. "Enjoy the adrenaline."

"I'm not dead!" Clutching his chest, Kelvin sat up and eyed the now-much-more-crowded server room. "And there are more of us."

"Oh, he's a quick one," Kalliope said.

"Long story short, the rescue actually worked." Jim hooked a thumb over his shoulder at Kalliope and the other two. After escaping, they'd learned that the boy's moniker was Tweak and the other girl's was Penumbra. "Now we keep going."

"Going where?" Kelvin asked.

"Good question."

Jim took Kelvin's arm to help him stand.

"Jim," Kelvin said, stopping him. "Actually, everyone. I'm . . . I'm sorry. For everything."

"For what? Nearly blowing us up?" Jim said. "Please. I've nearly blown up like a dozen times."

"I'm serious, Jim. I don't want to be that guy anymore. If I make it through this, somehow I'll get free of the Chaos Merchant. I'll make things right."

"Whoa, the Chaos Merchant?" Tweak said.

"Long story." Jim knelt by his friend–when had he started thinking of him as a friend?–and placed a hand on his shoulder. "We're good. Everyone here's got baggage. But one thing at a time right now, okay?"

Kelvin considered, then gave a reluctant nod and let Jim help him up.

"I can't believe I'm the one saying this," Jim said. "But we need a plan."

"Agreed." Eli gestured to the younger heroes. "We're a larger team now, so we'll move more slowly. Which means we need to plot our next move more carefully."

"Great," Natalie said. "Our next move to where?"

It was like she'd asked the silence, because silence was the only thing that answered her. Tired, beaten, stressed, they all looked to each other as if hoping someone else had a grand, inspired idea.

"Well," Zoe began, hesitant. "We already sort of cleared the way along one path. Should we retrace our steps? Pick up where we left off?"

"The path of least resistance," Eli said. "It might work."

Jim's memory flashed back to something Geometron had said. In her attempts at taunting him, she may have actually given something away. Something important.

"Wait," he said. "Geometron said all the obvious paths were deathtraps. But there's one that she said no one will find. Hidden like buried treasure."

"At least she wasn't cryptic about it," Zoe said sardonically.

"Buried treasure," Kelvin said. "Kind of an oddly specific description, isn't it?"

"Agreed," Eli said. "But there is nothing resembling buried treasure on the Lighthouse. I would know about it."

A dozen details coalesced in Jim's mind–clues he'd absorbed without even realizing it–and he *knew*.

"The Reliquary," he said. "You're used to it being there, Eli. For anyone else, that room is filled with treasure. Dangerous treasure, but still. When we were there, I sensed a blank spot behind the wall. A place devoid of all power. Before, I thought it might be where they hide the most dangerous relics. But could it be part of some secret path?"

All eyes turned to Eli, the Custodian, who must know every inch of this place, every nook and cranny and shadow. But this time, to Jim's surprise, Eli seemed lost. Confused, even, as if he had trouble processing the very idea.

"I . . . I . . ." he tried, then stopped and tried again, touching his temple as if he were getting a headache. "I don't know. When I think about that spot I . . . can't remember."

A confused Eli ranked pretty high on the list of weird things they'd encountered today. Jim couldn't dwell on that, though. Delay and indecision would be the death of them all. But if he insisted on testing his theory, could he be leading them into another trap? He vacillated, afraid to do something that would endanger his friends again.

Sheepishly, Kelvin raised a hand. "I know I shouldn't get a vote, given . . . well, you know. But before, we had no idea what to do. Now we have one idea. Shouldn't we at least give it a try?"

Slowly, one by one, everyone nodded. They weren't confident nods, but Jim wasn't any more confident, and it was his idea. But since they were placing far more trust in him than he deserved, and since Eli seemed out of sorts, maybe he should fake a little extra certainty.

"Okay," he said, mentally stepping off the ledge. "Here's what I'm thinking."

TWENTY SEVEN

ONCE again, the floor of the Shran tube dug into Jim's knees. He grimaced. This was still the best way to get where they were going–simple, straightforward, and hidden–but he didn't have to like it.

Crawling beside Jim at the head of the team, Eli noted his discomfort. "How do you feel?"

"Like someone hollowed out my insides with one of those apple corer things. What do they call those?"

"Apple corers."

"Right. So, that."

Exhausted didn't begin to describe it. Jim had never even thought of channeling that much electricity before. He still hadn't admitted this out loud, but when he grabbed those cables, he suspected the surge might kill him, and was as surprised as anyone that it didn't.

At least he wouldn't have to crawl forever this time. They were only sneaking to the docking bay level. There, they would exit and follow the donut-shaped corridor until they came to the Reliquary.

"At least we're moving forward," Eli said. "Thanks to you and your plan."

"If we survive, you can talk the Spectrum into making a black cape for me. Not to fight evil or anything, just to wear around the house. They look super comfortable. Give a white cape to someone else. I could not pull that off. I'm totally an autumn."

Eli almost responded, but seemed to reconsider at the last moment. He paused, as if switching gears. "We haven't really gotten to talk since being trapped in that room. Since your confession."

"I suppose not."

"I can't help wondering now why you're here."

"I thought I made that pretty obvious."

"I mean, why you're really here. Is it only to find the truth about your sister? Because I question whether knowing will be enough–even if it leads to finding her alive. After learning the truth, whatever it may be, will you really be able to go back to life behind your bar, hiding among the bottles?"

Jim affected a shrug as best he could while crawling. "Not really sure what the alternative would be."

Eli was pensive for a moment. "The truth has a way of changing things. Changing people. You chose the life you're living for specific reasons . . . but you could do so much more. Be so much more."

Jim side-eyed the Custodian. "Please say you're not trying to recruit me. I heard that sales pitch ten years ago when they gave it to Summer. We all know how that turned out."

"I'm not suggesting your true path leads here. Only that it diverges from the one you're on now. If what I suspect about you is right."

"And what would that be? I'm not guest starring on *Days of Our Lives*, I don't care how many times they ask."

"I suspect," Eli said. "That there's far more to you than the jester you show the world."

Jim had no response for that, no defense. The words had struck him right between the eyes. He studied the floor.

"So, not a sales pitch. Merely an observation," Eli concluded. "And a hope, I suppose."

Their arrival at the hatch saved Jim from having to change the subject again. Instead, he craned his neck to look back at their ever-growing team.

"Everyone ready? We'll be out in the open now."

"Ready!" Natalie replied with her usual vigor.

Hatch open, Jim crawled out and made way for the others. Tweak, the last one out, closed the hatch and they set off, following the corridor's wide donut-shaped curve.

"Next stop, shiny stuff," Jim announced.

"Shiny stuff that we will *not* touch," Eli said. "Because that's not what we're here for. Right?"

"Sure. Though, there is that glowing PB-and-J sandwich, and I haven't had a snack since–"

"That would not end like you hope," Eli said.

Jim prepared a comeback, but stopped short. Exhausted as he was, he only sensed the change an instant before it happened. He exchanged a fleeting glance with Eli, who must have felt something as well.

"Run!" Jim said.

Too late.

The blast doors in front and behind them snapped shut, closing off a fifty-foot segment of the corridor with the team trapped inside. Jim was about to command the doors to reopen when part of the ceiling imploded. Cacophonous sound and flying debris filled the space, the shockwave knocking Jim and Eli onto their backs.

A beam of cold shot through the hole in the ceiling. Acting quickly, Natalie tossed up a dome of stone to shield herself and the three rescued kids. The cold solidified around them, encasing them in a giant block of ice.

Solstice appeared, screaming bloody threats of vengeance while razor sharp spikes of ice burst from her hands to fly in all directions.

Before she could reach the floor, Zoe leapt to meet her in midair. Sheathed in blackness, she moved almost faster than Jim's eye could track. There was a clash, a flurry of clangs and thumps and grunts. Then, as Zoe somersaulted and dropped lightly back to her feet, Solstice hit the floor and crumpled like a rag doll.

"Heh. She's out *cold*," Jim said.

Climbing stiffly to his feet, he helped Eli do the same.

"For someone who hates puns," Eli said. "You make more than your share of them."

"When will she learn?" Zoe said. "She's by far the least threatening of–"

An ancient shield flew from the hole and slammed into Zoe's flank. She spun like a top and dropped hard onto her back, then kicked back up to her feet with impressive speed. Though, by the way she clutched at her ribs, Jim could tell that had really hurt.

As Zoe drew a shimmering black sword–the sword, Jim noted, that had been in the Reliquary–Millennia dropped through the hole to land heavily on her feet. Ancient armor gleaming, Chinese broadsword in hand, she aimed a scowl at Zoe that Jim had seen her inflict upon villains. It never went well for them after that.

"Oh, crap," Jim breathed.

Millennia said nothing. She marched up to Zoe and started swinging.

"Can you do anything to help?" Eli asked.

"They're so close together," Jim said. "In my state, whatever I do might hit them both. Maybe Kelvin could . . . hey, where's Kelvin?"

Staccato clangs of steel on steel filled the space, pulling Jim's attention. If it wasn't a life and death situation, the display of skill would have dazzled him. The two fighters circled each other, all their limbs constantly in motion, a ferocious dance of parries and strikes.

"What, no threats?" Zoe taunted the hero. "No chit-chat?"

"You know why I'm here," Millennia said.

With a *hyah* cry, she came within a hair of lopping Zoe's head off. They parted for an instant, then clashed again.

"Never seen that move before," Zoe said.

"I learned it before your grandfather's grandfather drew breath."

Zoe feinted with her blade, flicked her free hand, and a flash bomb burst in Millennia's face. Zoe used the split-second of surprise to slice across her opponent's forearm, hook around her broadsword and send it flying. The weapon clattered to the floor, out of reach.

Zoe grinned. "That one's newer."

Eyes narrowed, Millennia surged forward. Zoe swung Dark Sympathy. With two fingers, Millennia smacked the flat side of the blade and knocked the weapon out of Zoe's hand. Then she slammed her open palms into Zoe's chest, tossing her back as if she weighed nothing, to bounce off a wall and slide to the floor.

Zoe scrambled to her feet, only to come face to face with the unstoppable force that was Millennia. The hero slapped with her left hand, then her right, open palms cracking like thunder as they connected. Zoe's head rocked helplessly one way and then the other. Wavering, she attempted a limp counterstrike before she crumpled, dazed and half-conscious.

All business, like this was another day at the office, Millennia turned as her opponent fell and marched toward Jim and Eli. Jim braced himself to be next, but the hero barely seemed to notice him. She trained her focus solely on Eli.

"Custodian," she said. "You know we cannot suffer traitors. Not even you."

"It doesn't have to be like this, Fen," Eli said. "This isn't you—it's being done *to* you. Resist it!"

"Don't beg," she said. "Meet your end with honor."

His eyes betrayed a hint of sadness, but he stood straight, not even attempting to run. Without breaking stride, Millennia drew close to Eli and cocked back her fist.

Jim didn't think. His head filled with static and all he could do was act on instinct. No matter how dumb that instinct was.

He moved, placing himself between Eli and Millennia's wrecking-ball of a fist. Jim had just enough time to prepare for certain death, hoping it would at least buy Natalie time to break free and fight back.

If they say I died a hero, Jim thought in his last moment, *I'm coming back to haunt them.*

Millennia struck his chest with a hollow, bone-shaking *boom*.

They stared at each other, neither understanding what had happened. Jim didn't know which of them was more shocked. He had expected her fist to punch straight through his chest and come out through his spine. Instead, he only slid back a few feet, still standing and still alive.

At a complete loss, he looked down to find his torso intact. Although it throbbed like he'd been hit with a baseball bat, not a single rib was even cracked. And when her fist had connected, Millennia's arm had gone limp for an instant. Now her posture sagged and she glared daggers at him.

Even stranger, his insides were buzzing with a warm, energizing glow. He'd felt similar effects today, when fighting other heroes, but that had been subtle and easy to brush off as adrenaline from the heat of battle. Whatever this was, it was like nothing he'd even imagined. It felt like . . . possibility.

Millennia recovered, shouted a battle cry and charged. She punched him again, harder this time. The *boom* reverberated. Jim *oof*ed at the sledgehammer-like blow. But instead of dying, he felt like he'd taken one of Zoe's adrenaline shots.

"Ha!" Jim exclaimed. "Hey, if I survive a third hit, do I win a prize?"

With an exasperated huff, Millennia punched again. Apparently, that was all he could take, because his knees buckled and he slammed onto his back. Another sensation filled him—like he'd eaten a feast of whatever this warm glow was, and now he was full and couldn't possibly have another bite.

From the floor, he groaned up at the hero. "I'll take the stuffed tiger on the middle shelf, please."

Retrieving her sword, Millennia stood directly over Jim. She held the weapon high, blade pointed down at his chest.

"I know what you are now," she said. "So you will die first."

"Fen, please!" Eli said.

Wait, she knew what Jim was? What did she mean? *He* didn't know what he was, or what was even going on right now.

Yet, as Jim stared up at the hero, his perceptions raced forward. Everything around him slowed to a relative crawl. He blinked hard, disbelieving what his eyes were telling him. It must be a hallucination, something you got before dying. But even as he denied it, what he saw didn't fade. It only got stronger.

Inside Millennia, near the sternum, there was a ball of glowing green energy. It swirled and moved and flared like a living thing, like it had in the instant he'd seen it in Geometron.

Jim looked at Eli–he had a green glowy thing, too. Then Zoe–even unconscious, hers was there. Finally, Jim glanced down at himself.

Yep. Glowing green ball in his solar plexus.

All at once, he understood. He was sensing their parahuman power, and when attacked, he absorbed some of that power.

Maybe he'd always had this ability, but it was lying dormant this whole time. As Lode, he'd never battled other parahumans, which meant he'd never absorbed enough of their energy to activate it. But today . . .

Today, Solstice hit him with a freeze ray. Turbula hit him with a tornado. Road Rash tried to kill him with speed. Millennia tried to punch him to death. Each time, the strength of their attacks diminished when their power touched him, and instead he came away feeling energized.

Now it seemed he'd taken enough energy from Millennia that this ability had truly woken up. Jim could feel it now, as sure as the feeling that he had two arms. What he'd always been able to do with electricity, he could now do with other parahumans. See, sense, and absorb.

Jim wasn't just a Vessel for electricity. He was also a Vessel for the energy behind super powers.

All of which wouldn't matter in the next half-second, when Millennia plunged her ancient blade into his heart.

His sense of time raced back to normal. Eli was still pleading with Millennia for Jim's life. He didn't have time to pay attention to that. Instead, he cast his senses out for anything nearby, anything electrical that he could use to turn the tide.

His mind's eye traveled in an expanding sphere, passing through walls and into the Reliquary . . . where he found the perfect solution. Grinning, Jim extended his will, grabbed hold of what he'd found, and turned it on.

Or he tried. The motor groaned and clicked and stayed cold. *Oh, come on!*

Shoving Eli backward, Millennia commanded him to be silent, then trained her attention back on Jim. He tried to roll away, but as soon as he tensed, she delivered a swift kick to his face and pressed her boot into his gut.

"At least die with dignity," she said. "Not with–"

Someone shouted, and then Kelvin turned visible, clutching Dark Sympathy in both hands. He swung with all his might. The blade sliced through the air with a vengeance and struck Millennia's flank.

It bounced off her armor with a reverberating *clank*.

As the hero slowly turned her head to shoot Kelvin a you-did-not-just-try-that-with-me glare, Jim seized the moment. Setting his palm flat on the floor, he sent a series of commands through the Lighthouse's power grid, chief among them *Reroute* and *Recharge*.

Kelvin's eyes were as wide as saucers. "Um . . ."

Millennia beckoned to him, her eyes filled with gleeful murder. Falling back a step and dropping the sword, Kelvin turned invisible again.

Millennia scowled. "For an instant, I almost respected you. Hmph." Turning back to Jim, she hefted the sword and aimed for his heart once more. "Any last words?"

Recharge completed. The feedback flowed into Jim's senses like a soothing breeze. Gazing up at Millennia, he grinned. Because he knew something she didn't.

"Yeah," he said. "Enjoy the ride."

"What does that–?"

With power rerouted, with the recharge successful, Jim flexed his power and sent the final command.

The Kettle, the old Spectrum's armored transport, smashed through the wall and passed over Jim to collide full-force with Millennia. Caught off guard, she pancaked against the grille and could only hang on while it crashed through the window, toppling out of the Lighthouse and into space.

For a blink, Jim felt the vacuum's pull. Then the station responded and a shield slammed down to cover the hole. In the ensuing quiet, he lay there and allowed himself to breathe a sigh of relief.

"Oh my God," Zoe said, gingerly coming to her feet. "You killed one of the Spectrum."

"Millennia is the closest thing someone can be to immortal. She'll be fine." Eli offered a hand and helped Jim to his feet. "Thank you for risking yourself for me."

Approaching, Zoe stared in astonishment at Jim's chest. "I've seen Millennia punch through solid rock."

Jim smirked. "Hey, my eyes are up here."

Zoe laughed. "Idiot."

Kelvin reappeared next to them. "How did you survive that?"

Jim tried not to stare at the green glow inside each of them, now ever-present in his vision. "I . . . took some of her power when she hit me. Apparently, um, that's a thing I can do? I went inactive before testing myself against other parahumans. Maybe this was always there, waiting for me to find it."

Any response was cut off by a heavy sound, like cracking glass. Oh, right, they had teammates to free. As they turned to Solstice's trap, huge spikes of shiny black stone burst through the ice. The block cracked and then shattered, falling in chunks. As the stone receded, the four heroes leapt out with fists up, ready to fight.

"Aw man, you guys won already," Natalie said. Then she saw the hole in the Reliquary, and the shield over the window. "What happened?"

"Jim beat Millennia!" Kelvin said.

"Whoa, seriously?" Natalie said. "Jim, you're the man!"

The rescued young heroes stared at Jim in awe, which gave him the willies.

"No. No. There is no admiration allowed here. I'm a bad man. Zoe fought her. Eli reasoned with her. Kelvin distracted her. Otherwise, I'd be a shish kebab. Let's get moving, shall we?"

Turning, he started through the hole and into the Reliquary. The team followed closely. They weren't asking more questions, which was good. There were better things to worry about.

Besides, he needed time to process this. What did it mean? Did it have to mean anything? True, discovering a dormant power felt unexpectedly good, but he wouldn't need it after he got his answers and went back to his life. No matter how curious he was about how it worked, or what he could do with it, or nothing because it didn't matter and shut up.

"By the way," Zoe said as they walked. "*Enjoy the ride?* Seriously?"

Jim held up his hands. "Hey, when you're in mortal danger, you get points for even having a catchphrase."

Inside the Reliquary, he led them through the maze of glass-encased wonders, a swathe of them now toppled or smashed thanks to his stunt. This time, he barely spared them a glance. The bigger goal drew near.

He stopped at what appeared to be a random stretch of empty wall. An electrical blank spot sat behind it. Only, now he could see that it wasn't blank at all. Behind the wall, that empty space was wreathed in energy. *Green* energy that started here and stretched all the way down the length of the Lighthouse to pool at the very bottom.

A green line.

Jim shook his head. *Of course he knew.*

Somehow, Lord Neon had known that he would be able to see this. *It is the searching that will reveal the path.* He had said that right before all this began. Now Jim knew what the hero meant–if he hadn't gone through all of this to get here, he may never have discovered the ability that allowed him to see the green line. And now he knew beyond doubt that they were in the right place.

"This is it," he announced

"A wall?" Natalie said, sounding dubious. She patted his shoulder supportively. "I mean, hey, a wall! It's a nice wall, Jim. Good job."

Jim chuckled. "Thanks."

Expanding his senses, he probed for a way inside whatever this was. *There*–an activator button, hidden so that you'd only find it if you knew where to look, and what to look for. Jim pressed his power against it. A wide section of the wall slid open.

"Whoa," Zoe breathed.

The light from the Reliquary only penetrated a few feet. Darkness shrouded whatever lay beyond. No matter how ominous it appeared, though, Jim knew it must lead to where they needed to go. Where *he* needed to go. Whatever was going to happen next, it waited for them beyond the shadows.

Summer would have loved this.

Despite their grim situation, Jim couldn't help wearing a private little smile at the thought. Riddles? Secret doors? Some faceless evil pulling the strings? She would have eaten this up, and she would definitely have been the first to step through a mysterious doorway into the unknown.

"For Highreach," he whispered. "Always."

"What was that?" Eli said.

"Nothing." Jim put thoughts of Summer away for the moment. He needed to focus on whatever was about to happen here. With a deep, settling breath that didn't work at all, he made himself move. "Okay. Here we go."

One step. Then another. He crossed the threshold with the team at his back.

The wall slid shut behind them. Jim kept moving forward.

The darkness enveloped him.

On the deepest level of the Lighthouse, there was a room designed to be forgotten.

Inside that room was a containment apparatus–the only one of its kind–and suspended within it was a woman.

For the first time in a decade, she opened her eyes, and they were filled with relief. After so long, salvation was drawing near. Soon she would be free.

"Finally," she said. "My brother comes."

TO BE CONTINUED

If you enjoyed
WORST HERO EVER
the story continues in . . .

WORST TEAM-UP EVER
by
Archer Thorn

The only thing worse than a hero is a team of heroes. Jim Riven knows it, and the Spectrum–the world's most super special hero team–is proving him right. The Dare should have been a simple competition for recruitment, but these geniuses let someone corrupt their minds and turn it into something far more lethal, ironically forcing Jim to work with a bunch of misfit wannabes to survive. Although, the half-reformed villain is pretty cute, but whatever.

Now they've found a path to the endgame, and to what Jim's been searching for all along–the truth about what happened to his sister, the hero Lock. They just have to get there in one piece.

But the Dare is only the first move in a much larger game, and the enemy's final gambit could break the world. These oddballs might be the worst team-up ever, but right now they're all humanity's got. As the hunted become the hunters, it's up to Jim and his band of wannabes to confront the evil force behind it all, and do what the Spectrum cannot. What Jim swore he would never, ever do.

Save the world.

Want a free short story set in the
BLACK CAPE UNIVERSE?
Get your copy here . . .
www.ArcherThorn.com/freestory

ABOUT THE AUTHOR

ARCHER Thorn was born in the same city as you, on the same day, in the same hospital. In the room next to yours, his mission began. He has hunted you day and night for your entire life. When you finish this book, he will be standing behind you.

Run.

GLOSSARY

Aethyr
Most people don't know, and the ones who do aren't talking.

Apex* / "going Apex"*
*definitions redacted

Capes
No parahuman on Earth wears a cape. Except for the Spectrum. This is not official law, but hero and villain alike respect it as a cultural rule. Those who would prefer not to respect it still do so, lest they run afoul of other parahumans who don't take kindly to their attitude.

Faraday Parahuman Power Scale
The rating system by which a parahuman's energy output is measured. The higher the rating, the more powerful a parahuman is considered to be. This rating is independent of the energy's utilization, i.e. the powers that it fuels. The energy itself is not specific to any defined ability. A parahuman consumes this energy like calories, "burning" it as they wield their own particular powers (described in terms of class and sub-class). The more energy there is to "burn," the more powerful those abilities become.

The scale is organized in a decimal system, with these generalizations:
0.0 – Normal humans
0.1 to 0.9 – weak parahuman
1.0 to 1.9 – from weak to low-but-capable
2.0 to 3.4 – from low-but-capable to somewhat respectable
3.5 to 5.5 – actually respectable to mid-range to moderately impressive
5.6 to 7.0 – impressive to very impressive
7.1 to 7.9 – formidable to don't-mess-with
8.0 to 8.9 – seriously, walk away
9.0 to 10.0 – we used to have a moon, but they blew it up

Power output increases exponentially as one moves up the Faraday scale. With each decimal point increase, the energy output multiplies. A 4.0 parahuman is not simply twice as powerful as a 2.0, they are orders of magnitude more powerful. The power growth between ratings also rises with higher numbers. A 4.1 is a certain percentage more powerful than a 4.0, but a 7.1 is a greater leap up from 7.0. In addition to their core abilities, the higher a parahuman's energy output, the tougher and more resistant to threats and damage they will generally be.

When referencing a parahuman's rating on the Faraday Parahuman Power Scale, it may colloquially be referred to as a Capacity, a Faraday rating, a power level, or simply a number. The terminology is pretty loose, but everyone will know what you mean as long as you don't get too weird with it.

Is it possible to exceed a 10.0 rating?
See definitions for **Apex*** and **"going Apex"***

Parahuman Class
The application of a parahuman's power, or the effects resulting from a parahuman consuming (or "burning") their parahuman energy. While that energy is the same for all parahumans, the

effects of consuming it vary from person to person. In general, the "output" or manifestation of an individual parahuman's power can be slotted into a class (some manifest more than one class, typically at higher levels), and one or more sub-classes. While this system of categorization serves as a way to quantify the basics of parahuman ability, there are many more possible manifestations and permutations than the commonly known ones listed here. Powers, and power combinations, can vary as much as the wielders themselves, and more are being discovered all the time. As such, what is considered the standard definitions of the most commonly observed abilities is a shifting baseline, often changing and growing with each subsequent generation. New classes, sub-classes, and harder-to-quantify abilities continue to present themselves, and may do so at any time.

The primary parahuman classes are currently understood to be:

Blaster – Typically ranged attacks, with powers focused into beams or other concentrated output and directed at a specific target area. Most commonly emanate from hands or eyes, but are not limited to them. The quintessential Blaster is regarded as a "glass cannon," able to deal out enormous damage but withstand much less.

Controller – Specializes in manipulation, often at a distance and/or across a wide area of effect. These are not typically direct attackers or defenders, instead standing back and affecting elements of their environment on a larger scale, often to help allies and/or hinder enemies.

Sensor – Deals in information, absorbing unparalleled amounts of it through their specific medium. Able to parse, analyze, and interpret absorbed information quickly, often drawing conclusions that elude non-Sensors. Typically, they also have greater access to the information noted by their unconscious minds, and can factor all of that seemingly unperceived data. Some Sensors don't only absorb information, they can also transmit it (such as with telepaths or faunapaths).

Smasher – The tanks of the parahuman world. Typically very strong and very tough, with the ability to absorb tons of punishment. Damage output tends to be less than a Striker of similar power level, but constitution is higher. Abilities tend to manifest in close proximity to the wielder. In contrast to Blasters or Controllers, who are more likely to apply their power across a wide area, Smashers tend to sheathe themselves in their ability, becoming human shields / battering rams / living weapons / bullet sponges, etc. While their abilities don't typically extend far beyond their person, the intensity with which they manifest is formidable.

Striker – Fighter class, dealing out lots of damage while being able to withstand a respectable amount. General toughness (constitution, damage resistance, etc.) is higher than Blasters, Controllers, and Sensors, but lower than Smashers. With the exception of the Sniper sub-class, abilities tend to be up-close and personal, melee-oriented, usually quick and hard-hitting.

Traveler – Travel abilities are often considered a secondary power. But for parahumans with a strong enough affinity, and the will to learn and use it creatively, a travel power can be capable as a main. The stronger a Traveler power is, the more pronounced the parahuman's ancillary enhancements will be in order to support it. For instance, an especially fast Runner will find that in addition to being fast, their body is able to withstand the force and strain of moving at incredibly high speeds (wind sheer, gravitational pull, etc.), while their mind is able to process information quickly enough to keep them safe while in motion.

Parahuman Sub-Class
A more specific definition of a parahuman's ability, describing the particular aspect of a power class that manifests when they expend energy. Like classes themselves, sub-classes are highly diverse, always changing and growing, and many defy casual classification when all of the nuances specific to each parahuman are considered. As such, what's considered common is expected to shift over time.

Blaster

Aethyr – considered theoretically possible, but never documented

Energy – Radiant, Solar, Thermal/Heat, Nuclear, Cosmic, etc.

Elemental – Air, Ice, Fire, Lightning, etc.

Force / Kinetic

Psionic – sometimes called Mindsnipers

Sonic

Controller

Aethyr

Bio / Organic – areas of influence can include plants, animals, themselves (such as shapeshifters), and other people. Most healers are a variety of this class.

Booster – specializes in Buffs, elevating or augmenting a target's natural attributes and abilities. Can be used on parahumans or normals.

Digital / Technological

Electrical / Electromagnetic

Elemental – Air, Water, Ice, Earth, Fire, Lightning, Solar, Thermal/Heat, etc.

Gravity

Force / Kinetic

Psionic / Mind / Emotion – sometimes called Dominators

Suppressor – specializes in Debuffs, dampening or negating a target's natural attributes and abilities. Can be used on both parahumans and normals.
Time / Temporal
Weather / Climate

Sensor

Telepath
Empath
Enviropath – sense and absorb information about the immediate environment
Intellect / Genius – super-genius, process information with superhuman speed
Mediapath – sense and absorb information from sources of media
Florapath – communicate with, and sense information from, plant-life
Faunapath – communicate with, and sense information from, non-human creatures

Striker

Brawler – enhanced hand-to-hand pugilism
Duelist – enhanced proficiency with martial weapons (swords, staffs, shields, etc.)
Sniper – enhanced proficiency with ranged weapons (bows, guns, shuriken, etc.)
Stalker – the ninjas of the parahuman world, able to operate with enhanced stealth

Smasher

Aethyr
Bio
Energy – Solar, Thermal, Electrical, etc.
Elemental – Air, Ice, Fire, Lightning, Earth, etc.

Mega-Strength
Stoneskin / Steelskin

Traveller

Dodger – typified by hyper reflexes and escapes from danger
Flyer
Leaper
Phaser – can pass through and travel within solid objects
Runner
Teleporter

Parahuman Power Augments
Some abilities manifest, not as core powers, but as augmentations or complements to core powers. For instance, a Striker with a Brawler sub-class is typically considered a pugilist, some variety of hand-to-hand fighter. A Striker Brawler who can sheathe their hands in flame and deliver fire punches would be described as a Striker Brawler with a Fire augment. Fire is not a power that the Striker wields or controls as its own thing. It only manifests as an addition to the core abilities of the Brawler sub-class. Sensor augmentations are perhaps the most common. For instance, an Electric Controller will likely also possess some level of Electric Sensor ability, allowing them to perceive in greater detail what they control.

Prism
A team of heroes working directly for the Spectrum. While not as revered as the Spectrum seven, they are also highly regarded and respected. There are seven Prisms in total, each one under the direct supervision of a Spectrum member. Every Prism is also a team of seven heroes.

The Reaches
The twin cities of Highreach (yay) and Cloudreach (ugh).

The Spectrum
The world's most famous team of legendary heroes. Always seven members, each wearing one of only seven capes in the world. Each cape represents a color from the visible light spectrum. Three original members remain on the team–Skypuncher, Millennia, and Lord Neon–while the other positions have changed over the decades due to death, retirement, or other circumstances.

Warded Zone
Safe areas where no battle will occur unless agreed upon by both sides. Any parahuman crossing into the shield's radius will receive a small psionic burst, alerting them telepathically that it is time to behave. Even when battle is agreed upon, no major damage or fatalities are allowed in a Warded Zone. These areas are marked by a copper shield. This agreement is honored by heroes and villains alike, and even the worst of them abide by it. Some codes you just don't break.

Velocity
Parahumans are not allowed to play in normal people's sports, as their abilities grant them an unfair advantage. So a new team-based game was invented specifically for parahumans only, to showcase and leverage their unique abilities. It quickly became the most popular sport in the world. A high-octane combination of football, dodgeball, and insane obstacle course.

Vessel
An ability so rare, some believe it is mythical and doesn't actually exist. Once a child's parahuman power manifests (most commonly between ages 8 and 11), their energy output will grow as they age, and will typically stop growing as they reach adulthood (most commonly between 19 and 22). That final Faraday rating will be theirs for life, and generally considered to be "their power level." Though a parahuman can cause minor fluctuations in their energy output, it will remain mostly constant.

Not so with a Vessel. Their Faraday rating is often on the lower side, but it is considered only their *base resting* power level. Vessels are able to absorb energy and use it to boost their power level temporarily, essentially becoming a stronger version of themselves until the absorbed energy is expended.

It is theorized that Vessels must absorb the type of energy related to their core ability in order to boost their power. For instance, a Solar Blaster who is also a Vessel would have to absorb sunlight in order to increase their power level, while attempting to absorb electrical energy would do nothing. However, due to the extreme rarity of the Vessel ability, and the unwillingness of Vessels to identify themselves for study, most suppositions about how the ability works come from anecdotal observation.